Chi'Raq Gangstas 4

Romell Tukes

**Lock Down Publications and Ca$h
Presents**
Chi'Raq Gangstas 4
A Novel by *Romell Tukes*

Romell Tukes

Lock Down Publications
P.O. Box 944
Stockbridge, Ga 30281
www.lockdownpublications.com

Copyright 2022 Romell Tukes
Chi'Raq Gangstas 4

First Edition September 2022
Printed in the United States of America

This is a work of fiction. Names, characters, places, and incidents either are products of the author's imagination or are used fictitiously. Any similarity to actual events or locales or persons, living or dead, is entirely coincidental.

Lock Down Publications
Like our page on Facebook: Lock Down Publications @
www.facebook.com/lockdownpublications.ldp

Book interior design by: **Shawn Walker**
Edited by: **Cassandra Barrett-Sims**

4

Stay Connected with Us!

Text **LOCKDOWN** to 22828 to stay up-to-date with new releases, sneak peaks, contests and more...

Thank you!

Submission Guideline.

Submit the first three chapters of your completed manuscript to ldpsubmissions@gmail.com, subject line: Your book's title. The manuscript must be in a .doc file and sent as an attachment. Document should be in Times New Roman, double spaced and in size 12 font. Also, provide your synopsis and full contact information. If sending multiple submissions, they must each be in a separate email.

Have a story but no way to send it electronically? You can still submit to LDP/Ca$h Presents. Send in the first three chapters, written or typed, of your completed manuscript to:

LDP: Submissions Dept
P.O. Box 944
Stockbridge, Ga 30281

DO NOT send original manuscript. Must be a duplicate.

Provide your synopsis and a cover letter containing your full contact information.

Thanks for considering LDP and Ca$h Presents.

Chi'Raq Gangstas 4

ACKNOWLEDGMENTS

First and foremost, all praises are due to Allah, The Most High. Shout-out to all the readers rocking out with me—in the FEDS, STATE JAIL, COUNTY JAIL, and the streets. Shout-out to Yonkers, NY, my bro Moreno, CB,YB, SG, Lingo, and Spay Hoe. Much love to my Brooklyn niggas, O.G. Chuck, love you. O.G. Gunny, I see you. Tails, and my Villa niggas. My Bronx niggas: y'all know the vibes. Big love to my NC niggas, and my south niggas from Alabama to Texas. Respect to my Chicago drillers.

Much love to LDP and Ca$h, for all the love and support since day one. Free da real and free your mind—we all came from the same struggle. It doesn't matter your color, age, or size—pain has no picks, but you can overcome anything in life, just stay ten toes down.

Romell Tukes

CHAPTER 1

Staring over the dark, dangerous city, Boss looked out of the luxury, West Loop, condo window in downtown Chi'Raq. For the moment, and for many reasons, he knew coming back was the best decision he'd made, plus he still loved the city to death. Nevertheless, having been in Miami for so long after leaving Chicago, he realized just how much the change had affected his mind.

Boss had a homie named Spike, a GD from the Southside of Chicago, and his name rang bells in the street. The two had grown up together but he'd moved South East. Today, he had plans to meet up with Spike and discuss the business arrangements about their dealings. He wanted to flood the city with keys and he knew Spike was the man to get rid of them; however, trusting Spike would be the hardest part overall, because, friend or foe, he knew how the Chi'Raq niggas got down.

His mom was in Haiti with his Uncle Luc, handling business, while Lil BD was in ATL laying low.

Looking back on his life as he sipped on Henny, he still couldn't believe how fast things had changed since meeting his grandpop, who had later passed away. With none of his day-ones there with him, things seemed different, especially after Animal had turned him down for a snake bitch like Chole. All he had was Lil BD, his little brother, and even *he* had been keeping his distance down in Atlanta. Boss wasn't mad at him though, because he knew his brother had gone through a lot the past year.

Getting adjusted to his new life was the hardest part of it because he didn't know a thing about his uncles moving drugs on that type of level.

Lav was playing his role and doing the right thing but his Uncle Louis had turned out to be a different story. His mom basically told them Louis was out of the family, nobody had even shed a tear. To Boss, family was everything, so when someone went against it, the result was an all-out war.

In a few minutes, Boss was going to meet Spike in the trenches, a place he missed. Even though being back in the city felt like home, he still felt a black cloud over him. Flooding the town with drugs was his idea, because Chi'Raq was a gold mine if a nigga made it out alive and stayed out of jail.

Spike had an army and he was known to make some real money, but his biggest issue was the fact that he lived a dangerous lifestyle.

SOUTHEAST, CHI-TOWN

"NIGGA, BAG THAT SHIT UP a little faster," Spike told his young boy, Swerve, as two niggas in the trap house got ready for the long day ahead.

"We almost done, bro, on gang," Gun, Spike's fifteen-year-old cousin and shooter stated.

"Well hurry the fuck up," Spike told them, before walking to the back room to call his baby's mother about the child support money he owed.

Spike was a high-ranking GD in the city so he could go anywhere. He was from O-Block on 63rd not G4th, but he fucked with a lot of niggas from that side, even though they were all BD, his rivals.

Growing up he looked up to the Chi'Raq Gangstas— they turned the city up and Boss' name had become a legend overnight, but he'd earned his stripes in the field.

Spike's life had always been rough—even as a kid he was in and out of jail for shootings, drugs, and being nineteen years of age, he'd already miraculously beat three murder trials.

At the moment, the beef in the city was crazy between his crew and Spanish gangs like the Latin Disciples, Manias, and the Satans.

His rival, Juball, was one of the top niggas in Chi'Raq for the Spanish gangs, and they had been going back and forth killing each other's people day and night.

Spike's plug was a Vice Lord nigga he hated, and if shit went right with Boss, he'd have a big surprise for the plug.

When Boss had gotten in touch with him, Spike couldn't believe it, because word on the street was Boss had been killed by the police— and there were more crazy rumors about the King of the Rag.

As he waited by the window, Spike looked outside at his goons selling work and waited on any OPPs to slide through since they usually did. *Boss should be coming any minute,* he thought.

SOUTHEAST, CHI'RAQ

BOSS DROVE DOWN SPIKE'S BLOCK in a black Bentley Coupe with tints, and his Glock lay in his lap. Being back in the field felt so natural, and he loved to pull up to the block where niggas were posted up, selling work, and chasing the bag.

As he pulled up and parked in front of the building where he would meet Spike, he saw little niggas clutching and reaching, ready to bust.

He climbed out of the car and six niggas smoking weed slowly approached him. Noticing the two Cuban chains and the Plain Jane Rolex watch he was wearing, he was sure they thought they had a lick.

"You from over here? You gang?" a tall, young nigga with tattoos all over his face probed.

"I know you?" Boss replied. He was ready to give the little niggas whatever they were looking for—in broad daylight. He knew the young cats in these days and time wasn't playing, and neither was he.

"Nah, but this Spike block and if you ain't one of the guys then—

The tall kid's words were cut short when Spike rushed out of the building. "What the fuck you doing, nigga?" he shouted, before slapping the shit out of his best worker.

"Damn, bro, I thought he was a opp, bro! What the fuck?"

"Nigga, you know who this is?" Spike asked.

"Nah," the kid said, rubbing his face.

"That's Chi'Raq's finest gangsta, dumb ass nigga! Now get the fuck off my block before I kill yo' ass or send the get-back gang at yo' ass," Spike said in a raised tone. The kid followed orders and quickly bounced.

Boss and Spike chopped it up on the block for a few hours before making business arrangements to get money.

CHAPTER 2

MIAMI, FL

It was a nice sunny day out in the South Beach area. People rocked bikinis and G-String outfits as if it were nothing. As she did daily, Chole lay on the beach getting a nice tan to keep her skin polished. Since working out at the gym, Chole's body was looking tasty, like a snack. Since Thriller had been doing his thing and handling the drug transactions in Palm Beach County, life was good for her.

Selling drugs in Miami was the only thing she could do because Lau and the Haitians had the 305 doing backflips. Even though she had a concord there, Chloe barely came out to Miami since she knew Boss could strike at any second. The beef with the Haitians was still light and she wasn't about to be caught lacking in the streets.

Killing, and living the luxurious life, was all she knew, but lately, she'd been on chill-mode because she was starting to see a lot of money coming from Palm Beach.

Hitter was doing his thing and helping her network grow, but what Chloe really wanted was a piece of Miami yet she knew a lot would come with that. She still had goons and shooters on the payroll but not enough to go against the Haitian Mafia. What she needed was some strong help and a new ally—*if* she ever planned to go to war with Luc and Janella again. Everybody knew how dangerous Janella and her family were, and knowing their status in the game, Chloe knew she was blessed to still be breathing— becoming their OPP would come with deadly consequences.

In a few weeks, she would be having a big meeting with a Mexican cartel boss to talk future plans about business.

As she lay bathing in the sunshine, deep in thought, her phone chirped informing her of an incoming call.

"Hey, baby," Chloe answered Hitler's call on Facetime and she could tell he was driving somewhere in his Coupe.

"Where are you at?" Hitler asked.

"The beach."

"I should've known, babe, but I'm on my way to meet Rush and his boys—I don't like that nigga." Hitler was referring to a worker Chloe had found in Palm Beach.

"Put your feelings to the side. You a man, and only bitches do that," she stated.

"I'm good."

"Hope so. Don't fuck up my business 'cause he brings me a lot of money," she added, making sure Hitler understood his position.

"What-the fuck-ever," he said dismissively.

"His business matters to *me*! Now call me once the shit is delivered," Chloe said, before hanging up in his ear.

CHICAGO, IL: DAYS LATER...

SOUTHSIDE CHI'RAQ WAS QUIET AT 4 A.M., so it was easy for Spike and his goons to creep down the block to where his old plug stayed in a nice three-story house.

"Two of y'all go in the back and everybody else in the front with me, gang," Spike ordered, as he led his team of assassins on the night's mission.

Spike used to deal with VL, an old gangsta who had keys for the low, but VL would "herb" Spike, and he'd belittle him and try to play him every time he'd re-up. Every time he had to go deal with VL, the thought of killing him always crossed his mind, but he knew VL was his lifeline.

Now that Boss was supplying him, everything was great. His block had been banking big money. Dealing with Boss was a plus—not only were the drugs better, but he showed Spike love.

Using a jack he'd steal cars with on the regular, one of Spike's shooters slid in the front door with ease.

"Shhh, y'all play upstairs, bro," Spike said, walking through the living room area which led to another room.

As Spike made his way through the house, he noticed two of his boys coming through the kitchen and pointing toward a pitch-black hallway. There was a noise coming the room at the end and they had an idea who it was.

Spike entered first and his crew of Navy Seals tailed close behind, eyeing two bodies that lay in a king size bed—one leg hung off the side of the bed.

Whack! The sound of the pistol cracked VL upside his head and woke him up instantly, causing him to roll out of bed in fear.

"Wh-what the fuck?" An old, ebony-brown-skinned women with saggy breasts, popped up and tried to see what was going on, but the room was too dark.

"Don't cry now, fuck nigga," Spike said, as he inched closer to VL.

Beginning to get his vision back from the powerful blow he'd just received, VL looked up and in to the face of the culprit. "Spike, I looked out for you youngin'!" he said, while rubbing his head, "this some shady shit!"

"Welcome to Chi'Raq, nigga!" Spike laughed, but when he noticed VL's company doing a lot of moving on the bed, without warning, he let off four shots—*Boc! Boc! Boc! Boc!*

"Shit! Got-damnit!" VL shouted, as he witnessed his wife's murder up close and personal.

"Y'all go get the drugs," Spike told his crew, "He keep the shit in the kitchen sink and the hallway closet!"

VL's eyes grew as big as silver dollars and he wondered how Spike knew the exact location of his product. The one thing he knew for certain was somebody close to him had crossed him.

He rubbed his chin and scratched his head, a clear indication of being in deep thought. "How did you know?" He asked what his mental had probed long before the question had escaped his mouth.

"Yo' baby mama sold you out for some dick O.G. but consider it a good lesson.

"That bitch," he grumbled. VL hated his trick ass baby mama. She'd had him on child support ever since he could remember, but unlike most dads, he took care of all his kids.

"She was an eater too," Spike told him, "she tried to do the whole gang," he said, adding insult to injury. He shook his head and placed the pistol he'd used to kill VL's wife to VL's head.

"It don't gotta be like this," VL pleaded with tears in his eyes.

15

"Nah, it *do* though. See, you fucked up, big bro, and you gotta watch how you treat people," Spike suggested. Of course, he already knew it was irrelevant now.

Desperation was written over VL's face, and his voice trembled when he made his final bid—"I'ma make it right, I swear...come on, man," he begged.

"Nah, old head, it's over," Spike said, without the slightest hint of remorse.

Boc! Boc! Boc! Boc!—the noise of Spike's hammer was deafening as he triggered it and released four ear-piercing shots into the old man's head. Then, he tossed a blanket over the dead body before leaving the room.

His goons had been busy cleaning out the crib and gathering all the drugs and money VL had stashed.

CHAPTER 3

ATLANTA, GA

Lil BD's eyes slowly opened in his new five-and-a-half-bedroom mansion, which was located in the rich section of Buckhead. Moving to Atlanta had been the best choice he'd ever made, and shit was going good. He felt like a different man in his new comfort zone.

Getting away from Miami and the Haitian Mafia, made him feel like the stress he'd been carrying had finally been lifted off his shoulders. Months prior, there had been so much drama going on in his life, he'd seen enough to last him a few years.

Boss, Luc, and his mom Janella, lived for the family name, but Lil BD was starting to feel as if there was more to life and living besides selling drugs, killing, and gangbanging every day.

Leaving Chicago and moving to Miami had turned out to be the worst choice of his life, especially after losing Jenny. He knew he would never meet another bitch like her again because she had been a real ride-or-die type bitch from day one. With Hitler, his ex-best friend, on the top side now, there was no going back, and now that he'd moved to Atlanta, he planned to focus on living his best life.

The night before, he had gone out to a few clubs with two gang members and he knew they were down with a crew known as OTF from Chi'Raq. The clubs in Atlanta had to be the best, because Lil BD had a blast, unlike in Chi'Raq where everybody had to duck gun shots during a shootout.

After climbing out of bed, he put on his designer robe and slipped on his slippers then entered his private bathroom to take a shower and get ready for his morning

Living a new life felt strange to him but he was safe and happy even though he slept next to a Draco and a SK every night; however, life was still good.

Every day, he thought about his family's safety, especially his mother's, because, deep down, he knew she never wanted to take over her dad's position in the mafia but had no choice.

When meeting his uncles, he felt like they weren't really for him and Boss, but those were his personal feelings, so he'd never voiced them to Boss. Luc was mainly the muscle and the killer. Louis used to be the businessman of the family, but there seemed to be a black cloud over his head in Miami, and that's why he had to get away—by any means necessary. Besides, before he'd disappeared, he and the crew had been at odds.

NEW YORK CITY, NY

THE ALL-WHITE ROLLS ROYCE pulled up to the curb in front of Mikimoto, one of the most expensive jewelry stores in the city. Mikimoto sold quality diamonds that ranged from the most expensive diamonds like the Cullinan Diamond and the Hope Diamond.

Louis let his girl open the door for him like the true player he was—a bad ass Dominican with a phat ass and no stomach who could stop traffic on the busy New York streets.

For the past few months, he had been in New York doing big things with the help of his girlfriend, whose family was in the dope game heavy. Living in the Washington Heights section of New York, he was making a ton of money fucking with the Dominicans in the city.

"Papi, you want me to hold your pocket?" the woman asked, her dark-skinned, sexy Haitian lover.

"No, pick you out some diamonds," Louis told her, as she ran off like a kid in a toy store, ready to fuck some shit up.

Louis loved women who were willing to submit and obey to anything he required of them. He treated women like shit and that was the main reason he'd been single most of his life.

Being away from Miami was rough because Haiti and Miami had been his home since birth. He was at odds with Luc and Janella so that meant half of Miami and the whole Haiti would come for his ass. The idea of running had never crossed his mind, so he felt going to NYC would be a big step up and hoped his family would never find   him   there.

"Where is the jeweler?" he asked an older White man. The man stared at the diamonds around his neck and wrist.

"That's me, sir, how can I help you today?" the jewelry questioned politely. He had noticed the lady who had come in with Louis was picking out a lot of diamonds, so he knew Louis had money to spend.

"I want the best diamonds you got to put in my watch and chain." Louis pulled out a Black Card.

"We have the legendary, expensive Koh-i-Noor diamond that weighs a massive 105.6 carats. Its oval shape is magnificent," the jeweler explained. He watched as Louis ogled at the diamond sitting inside the high-secured glass box that sat alone on the counter.

"I want it."

"The cos—

"Get me the appropriate paperwork, including the details and warranty needed to make the sell, and you'll get a good tip." Leaving his Black Card with the owner, Louis turned and walked off.

CHAPTER 4
FREEPORT, THE BAHAMAS

The SUV tailed Maloney as they made their way to Condado Beach, a local beach with crystal-clear water. It was the designated place Maloney would meet his plug for the drug transaction.

Having the same plug for a few years, Maloney's dealings with the Costa Ricans were primarily based on dope—everything else came directly from his land where he grew his own cacao tree known as the Malvaceae. He had the best dope and coke in Central, South, and North America.

For months, he'd been hiking in and out of the mountains getting used to the nature again—something he loved to do.

One thing he knew for certain, nobody would look for him in the deep Bahamian tropical mountains. Shit, with the Haitians at an all-time high, he knew hiding out would only make shit worse, especially when Luc was on his bullshit.

Maloney's main target was Lil BD and Boss. Since he wanted them dead soon, he would have to get rid of them one by one. Louis was supposed to have brought Boss' and Lil BD's head to him, but it looked like that shit hadn't turned out too well for Louis, and he had idea that Janella had killed him.

Upon first meeting Louis a long time ago, he had seen the snake in his eyes, so he had always played him close. One thing he had to admit though, Miami and Haiti belonged to the Haitian Mafia.

A month prior, someone had reached out to Maloney saying he had a daughter. He did remember the beautiful, Black, short woman from New York. He'd met her on a short vacation he'd took around the same time the child was born.

One thing Maloney hated was a man who didn't take care of his responsibilities, especially his own child. So, he'd made plans to go to New York to look for the child since it had been awhile. Of course, going back to the states wasn't always safe, but Maloney had other business to tend to as well.

Pulling up to the beach area he saw the blue boat as it drifted to the dock carrying his drugs. Thiago was in charge of getting the drugs to him and he was a part of Vina's crew— the connect was a young woman who looked like a fuckin' kid. Maloney's devilish, evil eyes zoomed in on the boat, glad they were on time for once.

"Be ready ... it's time," Maloney told his crew, as they looked around with their guns drawn.

Maloney always rolled with a team of trained killers and ninjas who were prepared, and ready to kill, at any given moment.

The trucks parked close to the beach where the boats were docked, and the workers unloaded boxes off the boat and onto the white sand, for Maloney.

Thiago walked off the boat in search of the White boy with dreads, and when he spotted him, he smiled. While walking past his goons as they proceeded to unload, he realized Maloney's men had weapons, and for some reason, there were more of them than usual—they were extra deep in numbers.

"Maloney," Thiago greeted him in his strong, Spanish accent.

"My friend, Thiago, you're on time today ... that's a good look, my guy, how you been?"

"Fine! Your men brought weapons?" Thiago questioned him confusedly. He had never seen that before so he was nervous, because he wasn't a killer, just one of Vina's worker.

"Yes, today things are going to be a little different, but understand, it's nothing too personal, just business," Maloney said, and at the same time– *Tat! Tat! Tat! Tat! Tat!* —he pulled out a gun and shot Thiago in the head, killing him instantly.

Boc! Boc! Boc! Boc— Thiago's men returned fire at Maloney, but the shootout only lasted a few seconds. By the time it was over, Maloney had killed all of them and took all the drugs. He knew it would start a big war between him and the Vina, but he was ready. Robbing his connect took a lot of balls but he'd been searching for a new plug, and today had been the best time to get it over with before Vina connected the pieces to the puzzles.

Two weeks earlier, he had robbed another shipment Vina had sent to Brazil, and he had to kill his plug's crew as well as the Brazilians. Maloney knew if she ever found out what was going on, things would get really bad, really quick, and he knew the young bitch didn't play games.

MIAMI BEACH, MIAMI

IT WAS 8:30 A.M. AND DANILO SAT sipping on his morning cup of coffee. He was waiting for his daughter to get up and get ready for her first tour at the college she'd be attending.

There were two families in the D.R. who had been trying to step on his feet, and Danilo viewed such actions as a sign of disrespect. As a result, he'd sent Pablo out to the D.R. to take care of business because it needed to be handled ASAP.

Being in the game so long, Danilo understood that new hustlers would always try to enter the game and take whatever they could get.

Not one to be outmuscled, it was always Danilo's plan to come out of this as the top dawg. Living in his big new mansion in Miami Beach was considered his safe haven since the gates appeared to be the same height as prison walls.

The only side effect to living in Miami Beach was that his rivals ran the city of Miami, but he had his hand in the Broward County drug trade.

Luc controlled most of Miami and the two men had been at odds since the death of one of Danilo's daughters. When he gave his daughter, who was also his oldest child, he told Luc to protect her with his life.

The day his baby girl was killed, he vowed to kill Luc, as well his own family, and the day was coming soon.

Danilo went downstairs to have the maids prepare a meal so he could eat with his young daughter. Family was everything to the old man, but the new, younger generation didn't value family at all, and there were no morals these days.

CHAPTER 5

DELMAS, HAITI

Located in the heart of Delmas, a well-known area filled with drugs, murder, and robbery, Janella and Luc had a lowkey tunnel built in the basement of one of the traps, ran under Luc's authority. Running a city like Delmas took a lot of discipline, courage, and manpower because it was a very dangerous place.

"Did that money came through from Texas the other day?" Janella asked her brother, Luc. He was busy stacking the white keys of coke they kept in the tunnel, along with millions of dollars.

They had stash spots all over Haiti and Miami that only Luc, Janella, Boss, and Lil BD knew about. Louis knew of two but Luc took everything out of it just in case he tried anything dumb.

"I took care of that the same day, Sis, you know that, "Luc responded.

"Just making sure."

"Today is daddy's birthday," Luc told her. Since losing his dad, he hated when times like that came around.

"And I swear on daddy, I'm taking his head off," Janella said, as she wrapped shit up to leave.

SANTO DOMINGO, D.R.

PABLO, AND FOUR OF HIS MEN, had exited the car with big guns drawn. They were there to meet up with another drug dealer who simply went by the name *L*. L ran a big drug ring in-and-out of New York to the D.R. Working as the front man to Danilo's drug operations, he knew what to do, and of course, what not to do.

It was a busy day and Pablo needed to speak to Liman before seeing his cousins who moved weight for him in the slums.

Walking through the entrance of the nice sized house, his guest wasn't expecting him to show up, so it was a surprise visit.

Liman had no guards in his house, just family who were never there because they were usually at his other home.

"Lil BD is growing up and he's starting to see the bigger picture in life. He wants more for himself."

"Yeah, and that's understandable, but I need him here with us," Janella shouted.

"This is business and you know that."

"I do."

"That bitch Chloe got people in Palm Beach and I think we need to do something about it."

"We will be patient baby brother." Janella smiled because she hated Chloe for kidnapping her and making shit harder on her, but she planned to get back soon.

"Okay, perfect."

"Miami numbers have been rising since last month," she said.

"Facts, I peeped it last night."

"This fucker Louis is still somewhere missing in action."

"He can't stay away too long. I know his bitch-ass like the back of my hand," Luc said.

"He crossed us, so he's a dead man. I know we're gonna see him soon and when we do, he's gonna pay with his life."

"I try not to think about that shit, Luc."

"Yeah, but sometimes when I try not to think about it that's when shit be hitting me the hardest," Luc told her.

Early in the game, Luc had learned to take his emotions and consider them as most men do in life.

"I know the feeling, trust me."

"Boss called me the other day and he was ready for his re-up," Luc informed her.

"Already?"

"Yeah, I believe he got some shit going on in Chicago."

"Back to what he knows I see," Janella replied.

"He's a smart kid so I know he'll make good choices in life, especially when it comes to his business," Luc stated. He was seriously liking how far his nephew had come in the game.

"Boss still has a lot to learn in the game."

"True indeed."

"Lil BD disappointed me, Luc, I had big dreams for him," Janella said, still salty about Lil BD falling back from the family business, a few blocks away.

Pablo heard a voice coming from the basement so he made his way down there with the goons.

"Oh shit!"

"Don't be shocked." Pablo pulled out his gun swiftly as Liman made a phone call to his son.

"Pablo, I've been trying to reach you and your family because—

Boc! Boc! Boc! Boc— the bullets entered the man's chest and neck, dropping Liman in his chair just as Pablo left the basement, heading to his next mission,

Liman had been doing too much and he didn't have the respect to pay his dues to Danilo are Pablo. Respect in the D.R. would get a nigga killed, and Pablo didn't care how much clout a nigga thought he had.

Romell Tukes

CHAPTER 6

ARIMA, TRINIDAD

Kamla arrived back home just in time for a vital phone meeting with one of her lawyers from the states. That particular lawyer was mainly in charge of looking over her business and investments dealing,

Today was her late brother, Kevin's birthday, so she planned to get drunk and have a small get-together with another one of her brothers once he got back from Crown Point.

The island of Trinidad was her safe haven, home, and birthplace. Running a whole island beside the Tobago area wasn't an easy task.

She went to the room where the security guards usually congregated and noticed they were all on-point with assault rifles, ready to go at any given moment.

"Two of y'all fat fucks go outside and hold it down! Do y'all fuckin' jobs before I kill somebody in this bitch," she shouted, before slamming the door to leave.

As she walked down her hallway, she saw an old photo of her and Luc hanging on the wall. Since the divorce wasn't final yet, Luc was still her husband—at least on paper. Even though they hadn't been together in years, there was still a sense of chemistry between them, and it was probably something they would share forever; nevertheless, life's unforeseen situations and circumstances had led to their bad breakup.

A while back, Luc's family had killed her father, Imam Sa'id, and that's when the table turned and he'd become an enemy overnight. Having to be at war with her first love hurt, but she had no choice but to defend her family's name and honor. If Kamla let the Haitian Mafia run over her and disrespect her, other crime families would attempt to do the same, and the legacy her father worked so hard to build would've been tarnished. Aside from that, the local police and government had made it difficult for her crew to breath in the streets because they were constantly being hounded and harassed for drug money and dues. The chief of police wanted Kamla and her family to pay dues in the sum of a million dollars a week, but, of course, that was a dead issue.

She had lost twenty-two men in the last month alone, but that morning, her goons had caught up with the chief of police and the mayor's son, and now they were both tied up downstairs. Though she had important shit to do, she knew she needed to take care of the issue at hand, ASAP.

Walking downstairs, she saw two men tied up, ass naked on the floor, crying and mourning as if they already knew what would be next.

"You thought you could muscle me and my family, Mr. Mayor?" Kamla asked in a sweet voice.

"Please, we used to be close to your father. He's a good friend," the chief of police said, hoping to talk sense into her so she would spare his life.

"Bitch nigga, my pops never liked the police but I'm sure you know nobody fucks with my family," she said in a serious tone, before pulling out a small pistol. She shot both men in the head and killed them before going back up the stairs to take a shower. As she bathed, she released the negative thoughts that had been clouding her mind about the Haitian Mafia.

DADE COUNTY, MIAMI

LEXUS DROVE THE LUXURY MAYBACH truck through the luscious, rich neighborhood of Dade County where she lived alone in her big mansion.

Young Thug played through the car's stereo system and as she concentrated on the highway, she thought about what was going on in Colombia— the night before, her cousin had got killed by a rival cartel in Cartagena, Colombia.

Lexus had been running her own drug family ever since the death of her father who was killed at the hands of her number one enemy, a member of the Haitian Mafia.

She thought about killing all of them one by one, from Luck to Lil BD, but the one who would be hard to kill was Boss. Her history with Boss was different from the history she had with any other enemy because they were both still married and she had a love-hate relationship with him.

There was a lot of hurt and pain deep down, but she had a feeling Boss hadn't been responsible for killing her father but she had a strong sense his family did.

Mark waited for her in the long, narrow driveway in his Benz Coupe. She had to find out what happened because not only didn't she take losing family lightly, but someone stealing from her was a sign of the most disrespect there was.

The Alvarez Cartel been going at it with Lexus' family for years, but now there was a new leader of the family and Lexus felt as though he hated her guts.

Both families had strong armies but only one cartel could run Colombia, and Lexus knew she would have to do whatever it took to overcome the drug turf.

"Mark," Lexus jumped out in a white Louis Vuitton dress and heels, looking sexy and classy.

"Let's go inside," Mark said in a deep voice.

"It's that bad?" Lexus asked, seeing the expression on Mark's face as they walked into the twenty-two thousand-six hundred twenty-seven square foot mansion she'd gotten as a gift from her father before he'd gotten killed.

"The Alvarez's sent word to me saying that was only the beginning," Mark said, following her upstairs.

"It's been a war."

"No, they're saying everyday blood will be drawn until we're either dead or we throw in the towel." Mark spoke in a strong Spanish accent, unlike Lexus who talked like a Spanish hood chick from Bronx, New York.

"Fuck Alvarez! They want war? Let's give it to them fools," Lexus said.

"It's not that easy, Lexus"

"What the fuck you mean? They kill ours, we kill there's!"

"It's gonna be hard to get them, Lexus, especially since your father and I have been trying since the 1980's."

"Well, this is a new fuckin' era, so we have to find a new way, that's all, Mark, plain and simple. We're not gonna let them do us *any* type of way," Lexus told him. She was getting more and more upset thinking about how they had killed her favorite cousin just when he was beginning to make big money moves for the family.

"I think you should prepare for a big war," Mark stated, standing at the room door. Lexus began to undress in front of him as if she didn't give a fuck about his presence.

"Stay on point," she told him. "I want goons surrounding that bitch and I want all the spots we get money and shipments delivered to, guarded 24/7", she demanded.

"You sure?"

"Yeah, at least until we kill Alvarez because he's gonna keep striking until we go hard on him. I want a location for his whole family—from the babies to the old bitches. I wanna know where his grandma go to pay shit, and I wanna know what he eats for dinner, his favorite color, and even his dog's name," she snapped. "Shit, I wanna know his fuckin' dick size!" she shouted. Now, she had started getting upset with Mark because he was supposed to have been on the shit already since she was the boss and he was the family capo and enforcer.

"Okay, I'm on it, but I hope you know the drama you're about to—

"Mark, shut the fuck up and get the fuck out and just do your fuckin' job!" she grimaced in finality, and ended the conversation by walking off. She went inside her private bathroom and slammed the door closed, before stepping in the shower.

CHAPTER 7
KEMPS BOY, BAHAMAS

Maloney lay on the beach getting a tan because he hated his White skin and he always wondered why he was different, especially being a White boy. Growing up, he really disliked White people because they looked just like him. He watched two, sexy, darkskin women play in water, enjoying the beautiful, summery, tropical weather.

In a few days, he would be going off to the states, but at the moment, he was laying low letting two things worry him to death. His main source of stress was based on what he'd recently done to Vina because he knew it would be a big problem, and, of course, he was ready, but Vina wasn't the one to sleep on. Another problem he was dealing with was the news of him having a daughter who he had never met until earlier that day.

Going to the states would be deadly but he needed to handle his business with the grim reapers—Boss, Luc, and Lil BD.

Maloney needed an alley in Miami to link up with because his crew of well-trained niggas wouldn't be enough to go up against the Haitian Mafia. Tomorrow his flight would leave so he wanted to stay in the flyest hotel later that evening. He had already seen the goons out there setting up shop.

SOUTH MIAMI, MIAMI

LIL BD HAD GONE OUT TO MIAMI for the weekend. He had plans to chill in the BT'S Gentlemen's Club with Boss for his birthday.

"Nigga, I don't even do the clubs no more ... look at all the ratchet bitches in this bitch," Boss stated the sipped from her Henny on the rocks. He looked around the club and frowned disapprovingly.

"Bro, you used to be trickin' in the strip clubs in Chicago. Folk, you used to be up in the Gold Room," Lil BD said laughing.

"I was young then," he replied defensively.

"Whatever, birthday boy."

"How you like Atlanta because I barely see, or hear from you these days," Lil BD said.

"I love it, bro, and I'm living my best life out the way."

"True."

"I'm glad I fell back, bro, 'cause that life was starting to put a hold on my life and potential." Lil BD thought about getting back in the game daily but he knew it wasn't for him anymore.

"You do know that regardless of whether you're in the game or not, you'll always be a part of this family as well as someone people know." Boss respected his brother's wishes, when he got out of the game because he knew it was what Lil BD really wanted.

"I will never disclaim my bloodline, bro, but I had to make the best choice for me, bro."

"Facts. Shit getting crazy out here so I'm kinda glad you safe in Atlanta."

"What's going on?" Lil BD sounded a little worried but he knew that wasn't his life anymore so he usually minded his business.

"No need for you to worry. It's nothing we can't handle, bro, so let's just enjoy this night," Boss replied. Then he called two dancers over for them—one for each of them.

When Lil BD looked up at the dancer, he couldn't help but notice one of the women looked just like Lexus, and he couldn't help but think about her as the night went on and he continued celebrating his birthday.C

CHAPTER 8

PALM BEACH COUNTY, MIAMI

Mark went out to speak with his cousin Big Hulu. Though they were family, Big Hulu was his boy, and for the past few years, he'd been moving a lot of dope and coke for him.

Driving through a Latin neighborhood, he thought about the last conversation he'd had with Lexus about the Dominicans and the Haitian war. Having a major piece of Palm Beach was a huge achievement but there was still a large part of the city that was under the authority the blacks.

Big Hulu knew almost everybody moving weight around his way, so he networked with a lot of shakers and movers in the city except his OPPs, of course.

When Mark had first opened up shop in Palm Beach, Lexus hadn't been in total agreement, but now that it was prospering, she loved it and was happy he'd made the move.

Pulling into an auto body shop owned by Big Hulu, he saw a worker stripping down a car and fixing the rear bumper.

Mark got out and saw his cousin, Big Hulu's, big truck parked out front by the garage, so he knew his fat ass was inside, most likely eating.

"Big Hulu?" Mark yelled, stepping inside the establishment.

"He's in the office, boss man," a young man told Mark.

"Thanks."

Walking to the Big Hulu's office, he smelled Mexican food and he knew it was Hulu.

"Cuz!" Big Hulu shouted out, as he lifted his head from the bowl of Mexican food his girl had cooked the night before. The two workers who were in his office with him stepped out to give him privacy to talk.

"How's everything, Hulu?"

"I can't complain, cuz. I been going through a lot of bull shit dealing with the local gangs," Big Hulu stated, after wiping his mouth.

"Ain't you a Latin King or some shit, Hulu?" Mark asked, curiously— he knew his cousin was gang affiliated.

"Yeah, and my people been out there warring over turfs and shit."

"Y'all need more manpower?"

"Nah, we good over here, big bro. I just need you give me a few more days to get your money." Big Hulu saw the look on Mark's face.

"You know I don't play 'bout my money, cuz." Mark was about to reach for his gun. One thing everybody knew about Mark was, he would kill over his money, friend or family he had no picks.

"Cuz, give me a week. I got you. Things just been bad lately 'cause my crew took a big hit by the feds."

"And you still out there?" Mark smirked, knowing Hulu wasn't a rat and he would never fold.

"Mark, I have morals."

"I know but just have mine by the time I come back next week." Mark walked out and slammed the door behind him.

Big Hulu sat there thinking about his rivals and how the beef in his area was getting out of hand, but he was ready for it all.

NORTH MIAMI, FL

CHOLE WAS BENT OVER ON ALL FOURS getting fucked doggie style, and she was loving every bit of it.

Hitler pounded her back, feeling her warm, tight pussy wrapped around his penis.

"Ohhh shitt …," Chloe moaned, making herself cream more and more.

"I'm cummin'," he gritted out, as he nutted in her love tunnel which was always soaking wet.

"Yes, daddy," she slammed her ass hard on the dick as she tried to climax for real.

"Fuck." Hitler felt his body go weak as he came and he wanted to go straight to sleep.

"That was so good, baby."

"Facts, but how's the shipment looking for this week?" Hitler asked.

"Same." She responded in short simple words.

"I'm just making sure you know because Rush and them are ready for me as we speak," Hitler said.

"He'll be good this week so you can tell him that, but did you make them moves in Atlanta and NC?" she asked, as she lay down and admired her own breasts.

"I handled it."

"Okay."

"Look, I'ma run to the store real fast."

"Get me some smoke, baby," she told him. She got comfortable in her bed and thought of a way to carry out her new plan which was to take over Broward County and Palm County since Miami was already locked down under the authority of Luc, Janella, and Boss.

"A'ight, ma." Hitler left the condo with a Glock 10 on him because he wasn't trying to get caught slipping by the niggas in Chi-Town.

Even though Hitler was in Miami with Chloe and they were living their best life, Chloe had so many problems and mood swings, at times, he had no clue how to deal with things. Pushing all of that to the side for the time being, Hitler thought about his ex-best friend and who would kill who first.

Romell Tukes

CHAPTER 9

PALM BEACH COUNTY, FL

Hitler drove to a nearby Walmart parking lot to meet with an important business friend—a young man named Rush. Chole had met him first and thought he would be good for business.

At first, Hitler wasn't feeling it and then he started to see all the money Rush was starting to bring in for him.

The relationship between him and Chloe was uncomfortable at times because she was a boss, and Hitler felt like his women should treat him like a boss also. Since coming to Miami, he'd seen the growth in himself as a man, and a person dealing with life. Coming from Chicago to a new city like Miami, Hitler only had two main objectives—to get money and to kill Lil BD and Boss. Chloe had come along at a time when he felt alone and at his lowest point in life, and she'd been around ever since. When he let her brainwash him into doing whatever she pleased, his life had been turned upside down.

The car pulled up next to a sky-blue Charger sitting on big chrome, shiny rims. Hilter hated county niggas; he'd never understood them and didn't care to try.

Getting out of the car, he snatched a big shopping bag filled with bricks for Rush, and in return Rush had money for him.

"What up, dawg." Rush spoke first as he climbed out of the Charger with a bag filled with money. He didn't really like Hitler like that but he understood he was Chloe watch dog and muscle. When he'd first met Chloe in a club, he had no idea she was a plug on another level.

Chloe eventually sent Hitler to give him the bricks and shit but he didn't press the issue because he was focused on money and success, not a bitch.

"Everything here?"

"Facts, everything here," Rush shot back.

"I don't play when it comes to mine, believe that," Hitler stated proudly.

"You mean Chole's, 'cause from my understanding you just the muscle and delivery guy so I guess we all got a position," 'Rush expressed.

"You got a smart mouth on you, I see."

"Maybe."

"I'll be back in a week for the next move but next time pick a better location. This shit in the open," Hitler said, tossing the money he had to turn into Chloe as soon as he got back to the crib, in the back.

Hitler disliked Rush and every time he saw him he always had some shit to say about something. Luckily, the kid was bringing in a lot of money on the daily, and he couldn't fuck that move up or else Chloe would be very pissed.

Miami and Broward were big money spots and the only issues was that the Haitians and Colombians were the ones who had the cities on lock.

Hitler had really been thinking about going back home to Chi-Town to open shop, but with so much beef, his drug run would only last a few days.

LIBERIA, COSTA RICA

VINA SAT OUTSIDE ENJOYING the beautiful city of Liberia where she had a very large mansion near Santa Rosa Park in a quiet, rich area.

For Vina and her guests, her home was equipped with four main villa's to offer. One of the guest houses had been built with two additional bedrooms on the entry level with an en suite bathroom, a cinema room, and a gym. The exterior had both a spacious front and backyard, three outdoor pools, and there was even a well-groomed garden.

`Vina loved to work and practice the use of firearms. She'd shoot at her personal range a few blocks down the road, next to another mansion she owned.

With no guidance, she was just a child when she'd first got into the game. Her parents had died and everything they owned was left to her so she could hold the family down, and she'd done just that.

For a female who now controlled most of the drugs coming through Central America, being in the drug game wasn't easy. To earn the respect she deserved, she had killed a lot of strong kingpins and powerful people. Being a young female in the game, there was still a lot she needed to learn, but she became a true savage early in the game to show people she wasn't the one to fuck with at all.

Because she had a lot of enemies—some she knew about and some she didn't—guards patrolled around the front and back areas to ensure she was safe at all times. It was all a part of the game to have OPPs so she didn't mind, but what got her pissed, was when she gave someone a chance and they fucked her over. Crossing a women like Vina was the worst thing anyone could do because she took loyalty and good business to the heart.

Right now, Maloney was her number one target after he'd robbed her and did her wrong. She had a plan but Maloney was a smart nigga, and she knew finding him wouldn't be as easy as it sounded, but she never gave up on a target until the job was done.

Romell Tukes

CHAPTER 10

MIAMI BEACH, FL

Pablo arrived at Danilo's to have a sit-down with the boss in regards to some business arrangements about details in the D.R. and P.R.

Trying to get business right with other drug lords who bought from them, Pablo had been moving back and forth from Miami to the D.R. He hadn't seen Danilo lately due to his time in the other countries— he was off trying to make a way for his family by networking with other cities to take over.

The Porsche sped down the block into the gated community as rich, White people looked at him like he'd lost his mind driving through the neighborhood at such a high speed.

He pulled up to the crib and all the luxury cars which belonged to Danilo, were parked out front in a long line. The mansion was so nice and he loved the layout because it had four levels.

Walking through the double-glass doors, he yelled his uncle's name. He heard his voice as it echoed from the lower section of the house, the place where he'd always hide out.

The lower part of the house was fancy and large. It was his uncle's sport's and bar area, but he called it his dining area.

Danilo reclined in his Lazy Boy as he drank on top shelf liquor. "Nephew," he greeted.

"What's going on, Uncle?"

"Same shit, bigger toilets," Danilo stated back. He pulled a cigar from the humidor he kept them in to maintain freshness.

"I want to speak with Theodore." Danilo hated Theodore and Pablo noticed the look he'd given him at the mention of Theodore's name.

"I thought I told you to kill him," Danilo replied.

"Yeah, but I had a business plan I knew you would accept. Instead of killing him I figured he could be very useful to us.

Danilo frowned. "You figured?"

"Yeah, he offered us his whole city if we would supply him."

"Why not kill him then we take over his shit?"

"Because that would backfire on us."

"I didn't teach you to go against my word or demand, Pablo. You're getting too big headed," Danilo said.

"I was trying to think as a businessman, and besides, he's better to us alive than dead."

"You don't have the authority to make that choice so make that your *last* time. Do I make myself clear?" Danilo asked his nephew; about the young man he'd raised since a kid.

"Okay, it won't happen again, Uncle, I promise," Pablo answered before exiting the room. Now, he had to think of his next move since he knew he needed to figure shit out. Knowing his uncle well, he knew Danilo meant business every time he talked.

WASHINGTON HEIGHTS, NY

LOUIS LAY AT HIS GIRLFRIEND'S CRIB waiting for her to get out of the shower but she thought he was still asleep. The night before, Louis had gone out to a club to celebrate his birthday and the night had been long and crazy.

His girl had been acting weird lately but she'd told him she was pregnant so he figured that was most likely what it was—either that, or she was just a moody bitch.

Lying there, all he could think about was how dirty his whole family had done him, and he had it out for all of them—even Lil BD and Boss.

Staying in New York was a big change and he loved it. Nobody knew who he was or why he was even up there. He knew keeping a low profile was the only way to get by in the crazy city, and more importantly, he didn't want it to be too hard to blend in.

Louis looked over to his left when heard a phone ring. At first, he thought it was his phone, but as he studied it longer, he realized it was his girl's phone. He paid the phone no mind as he listened to the sound of the water coming from the bathroom shower. The cell phone continued to ring, which by now, had got his full attention.

He picked up the pink case that held her phone. Looking at the message, he read it and saw all the back-and-forth calls, to and from Texas, that had been going on for hours,

"Bitch!" he yelled, as he read the texts with wide eyes.

The texts couldn't be disputed. Louis jumped out of bed and reached for his FN handgun. There was no way he would let a bitch set him up. So, he ran in the bathroom and snatched the curtains back.

"Ohhhh shit, papi," she screamed at the sight of the gun.

"Bitch, who made you set me up?" Louis asked.

"I don't know her but she sent me the money through cash app."

"Bitch, you better think fast," he stated seriously.

"Her name was Jane or Janella, something like that," she cried out in tears, knowing her life was over.

Boom! Boom!

Louis shot her in the head and killed her— he watched her body collapse in the shower. Knowing niggas was outside waiting on him, he climbed out the escape window just before the door was kicked opened with four gunmen on the other side.

Luckily, he made it outside just before they ramshackle the crib inside-out looking for him. He knew the intruders had been a gift was from his own blood, Janella, and he had a feeling Luc had also been in on it. Now, he would return the favor and plan both of their deaths.

Romell Tukes

CHAPTER 11

SOUTH SIDE, CHICAGO

Heavy walked into the corner store with his boy, Bopy, his day-one since middle school.

"I'll be there in a few minutes, bro, but y'all better have my fuckin' money when I get there or somebody gonna pay," Heavy told one of his workers. He'd told Heavy he'd needed to bond himself out the night before, and he'd used Heavy's money.

"What that goofy nigga say?" Bopy asked, laughing. He knew how Heavy got overly emotional about his money.

"This bitch nigga think shit a game, bro, on gang," Heavy said, grabbing a few bags of chips because he had the munchies.

"I think he got booked last night with Black and Boy Bay," Bopy said, laughing in his boy's face.

"Fuck all that," Heavy puffed with a sad face.

Heavy was the cousin of Juball, the biggest drug dealer on the South Side. Juball had the city's gangs on lock— including the Latin Kings and Satan GD's. He was pushing big weight in the Spanish neighborhoods, which helped elevate his status in the game.

Heavy had been at war over blocks and trucks with two of the biggest gangs in the city known as the GD's and the Black P Stones. Beefing caused him to lose a brother and a few good homies on the journey.

"I heard the OPPs was inside Club Disco near Fulton River district with Mickey from the Snakes, on gang," Bopy said, as Heavy picked out a few snacks.

"Mane, that's why I never fucked wit' none of them niggas, on the gang," Heavy said, paying for their items, ready to head back across town to Englewood.

"Fuck them niggas, bro. Them niggas ain't even slide for Lil Troy and he was their main shooter, bro. Them niggas scared, talkin' 'bout they got back at them OPPS, gang. But they ain't do shit!" Arauture stated.

"Fuck Spin," Heavy said, walking out of the store. Not aware of his surroundings, two gunmen with black flags wrapped around

45

their faces hopped out of an old Cadillac with MP5's, HK's, and M4 clips spraying rounds.

Tat-Tat-Tat-Tat! Tat-Tat-Tat-Tat!

"Ahhhh!" Arauture screamed as bullets hit his upper body and caused him to crash into a nearby garbage bin.

Heavy saw another shooter arrive from down the street and he knew shit wasn't right because everybody was running as the man headed in his direction. When he realized it was Spin, he almost shitted himself while running across the street, fumbling for his gun.

Boc! Boc! Boc! Boc!

Never in a million years would Heavy have thought he would be so close to God, as he tripped over the curb and at the same time felt the bullets, from Spin's Glock .43 handgun, hit him.

"Got your bitch ass," Spin said standing over Heavy.

"Man, please."

"Nigga, shut your bitch ass up begging for your life," Spin laughed, as the roar of the sirens could be heard from a few blocks away.

"Bro, you know my mom," Heavy said, before his brains got blown out all over Spin—his two shooters ran off for dear life as if the boogeyman was chasing them then ducked down in an alleyway.

DOWNTOWN, CHI'RAQ

BOSS WANTED TO GO OUT AND GET a bite to eat from a restaurant in West Loop. He waited for Spin to show up so they could talk about the next pick-up and other future investments.

Today, he planned to bring Spin over, but normally, Boss would never disclose his primary location to anybody, not even his family.

Sipping on Grey Goose, he started to feel nice and tipsy. However, nowadays, he had tried not to go so heavy on the hard liquor since he knew what it could do to a person's body.

He had cameras all over the condo and he saw Spin coming inside the front lobby of the building where the guards were. For some odd reason, he'd been thinking about Lexus and how dirty the bitch was but he couldn't figure out why he still thought about her so much.

He opened the front door for Spin who was impressed by the fancy building though he'd seen it many times when he'd drive by. Still, he'd always thought it was just a regular corporate building.

"What's good, big bro?"

"'Sup, Spin?"

"Same shit with a bigger toilet," Boss shot back, full of smiles.

"I took care of that little issue I told you about."

"Spanish cats?"

"Well, *one* of 'em," Spin corrected.

"Good, so all is well, I assume?" Boss asked, pouring two glasses of Moët which had been supplied just for being a resident of the condo.

"Facts, my people are taking over Chi blocks and my goal is to have at least 50 percent of the heads in the Southside coping from me," Spin explained his plan.

"That's what I wanted to talk to you about today." Boss sat down and handed him a glass of liquor.

"Facts, let's talk, boss man."

Spin and Boss talked and plotted for hours.

Romell Tukes

CHAPTER 12

AEROPUERTO, COLOMBIA

Aeropuerto Internacional Alfonso Bonilla Aragón Airport was packed as Arauture from the Alvares Cartel got off the private jet, surrounded by airport workers and family.

Arauture was coming back from the trip he'd taken to the Virgin Islands. He'd gone to talk business with some very important people who wanted Lexus dead as well, but Arauture planned to keep it to himself.

Getting off the jet, two goons carried his bag to his truck that awaited him as he walked slowly to the car, conversing with his cousin on his cell phone. There were a few cars outside that he didn't recognize but he continued to walk and make his way to the truck without a care in the world.

The look on his guard's face said it all as he'd almost made it to the back of his truck before shots were fired.

Tat! Tat! Tat! Tat! Tat!— a gang of shooters came from everywhere, taking out his security team, as he jumped in the backseat yelling for the driver to pull off; unfortunately, the man was already dead.

Tat! Tat! Tat! Tat! Tat!— the bullets outside sounded like thunder during a summer storm. Arauture grabbed his handgun that he'd placed underneath the bar of the limo, for times like this. Arauture hadn't been in a shootout in a long time so he was extremely nervous.

The limo door flew open and he couldn't believe who slid inside, in a pair of high heels and a dress.

"Bitch!" Arauture yelled at Lexus before he pulled the trigger again and again, as she laughed out loud.

"Your so-called most-trusted goon took the bullets out for the same fee. That's why I tell people to be careful how you teach people," Lexus said, now showing her own weapon.

"Lexus we're family and it doesn't have to be this way. We can get money together," he said, staring at the barrel of the gun.

"Never heard you talk so nice," Lexus said, getting a good laugh out of all of the shit.

"I think we should talk," Arauture said, looking out of the truck windows—his men were nowhere in sight; however, Lexus' goons had the limo surrounded.

"Sorry, Arauture, but we're in too deep to talk it out," she said, emptying the clip in his face and leaving his body slumped in the chair for someone to come get him up.

Now with Arauture out of the way, she would be able to focus on her own business and her main target, Boss, who was out making a lot of noise for the Haitians all through Miami city.

Leaving the airport, she made a few calls to Arauture's people so they could work for her, which had all been a part of her evil, little plan.

***

Rowley drove a Jeep Wrangler with no door handles, and he always rode with a bunch of goons accompanying him. Being Kamal's brother, made shit hard because he always felt like he needed to top her.

Arriving at the house, which looked like something out of a horror movie, Rowley parked and his men got out and rushed inside of the rundown complex, which was used for stashing guns and killing people; things that fell in line with K-Do and his big cousin Rowley's type of work.

"K-Do?"

"Right here," K-Do yelled from the other side of the apartment. The strong smell of death filled the air throughout the place.

"What's this?" Rowley asked, looking at the man all bloodied up— his head lay on a chopping block as he begged and cried for his life.

"When did Haitians start coming all the way over here to shop for fish?" K-Do asked another hitman in the family who was bat shit crazy.

"He work for someone?"asked Rowley.

"He's not talking." K-Do was beyond frustrated.

"Give me that ax," Rowley said. She took the ax and wasted no time chopping off the man's wrist.

"Luc!" the man yelled out in pain, finally giving up who'd sent him.

"Luc sent you to do what?" K-Do wanted to know because he'd been there for an hour and couldn't get a word out of the man, but Rowley had gotten him to talk in a matter of seconds. If he'd had his way, he would've cut the guy's wrist off from the jump.

"He sent me over here with bombs so I could blow you up," the man said, before he passed out due to the amount of blood he'd lost.

Rowley shot the man in the head and killed him instantly, then he pulled K-Do to the side to talk about their new mission as if he'd done nothing.

Romell Tukes

CHAPTER 13

BUCKHEAD, ATL

Lil BD pushed the new all-white Bentley Continental GT manufactured and made by the British. He went to a big party at some new club in Atlanta called *The Doom* and it had just recently opened. He'd met a few niggas in the club from Zone 3 and Zone 1—they needed a plug, but Lil BD wasn't thirsty enough to get back in the game.

Driving home after a few drinks, he was feeling a little tipsy. Falling back from the drug game had to be the best thing he'd ever done in his lifetime, and it was worth it because he loved his freedom and life.

Everybody spoke to Boss about him giving up the game and his family ties but he had to stay in the limelight. He lived in a grand stone, 17,017 square feet internal living space, with four acres of lavishly landscaped grounds, a stone pool, guest wing, an attached four-car garage, and a bar and wine room.

Lil BD pulled into the driveway of his estate and parked next to his motorcycles and Bentley truck he'd copped two days before. Climbing out of the car was a task because he couldn't even stand up straight due to Henny that filled his liver and kidneys.

Walking into the house, a noise on the top level caught his attention but his vision was blurry because he was so fucked up off the liquor.

Two men dressed in all-black jumped down from the upper level with guns. When Lil BD realized it was an ambush, shit happened too fast for him to react, and a bullet hit him in the arm, from the side.

Ninjas came from everywhere, ready to fight using their skills of martial arts, including ninjutsu. Some men had guns and swords, and others brandished star knives, and nunchaku— a weapon used in martial arts made up of two sticks joined together at their ends by a rope or short metal chain.

Lil BD was rushed by two men who released powerful kicks that knocked him down to the floor before they surrounded him.

When he looked up, there were ninjas everywhere and four had weapons aimed directly at him, ready to eliminate him without a second thought.

Tat-Tat! Tat! Tat-Tat! Tat! Tat!—bullets entered the house from all directions while another group of gunmen entered the house simultaneously—*Tat-Tat! Tat! Tat! Tat!*

Lil BD saw the gunmen and then a women dressed in all white entered inside the mansion wearing a facemask. The gunfire went on for a few more minutes and when it stopped, the women approached Lil BD.

"You okay?" she asked with a Spanish accent.

"Yeah, I'm straight," Lil BD replied. He gazed up at her, but due to the mask, all he could see was the beautiful color of her eyes. Then, like magic, she turned to leave just as quickly as she'd come. Realizing that someone he didn't know had just saved his life meant a lot to him, and the mysterious aura she possessed piqued his curiosity all the more, so he had to know. "What's your name?" he asked.

"Vina."

"*Vina* from where?"

"You find out, trust me," she replied, before leaving with the team of assassins she had brought with her.

When Vina exited, she'd left a bunch of dead bodies on the floor, and Lil BD was left with a bullet stuck in his arm.

"Fucking bitch," he mumbled out, and in pain. After he'd got up, he bent back down and snatched one of the dead gunman's mask off and revealed a black man with dreads. Lil BD could tell the man was Jamaican or from the Island.

Staying in Atlanta at the moment was the worst thing that he could do after the home invasion, so he called Boss as he ran to his safe to get some important papers.

MIAMI, FL

Riding with Pablo as he drove her to school, Christina bopped her head to the music. Trying to annoy the fuck out of him by listening to the *Pop Smoke* song, she looked at him and asked, "What you know about love on the radio?" She smirked.

"Please," Pablo answered *clearly* annoyed. He turned the volume down because she was driving him crazy.

"What?" Christina asked as she looked at him again and then quickly turned away as she tried to contain her laughter.

"Shut up."

"Whatever," she shot back.

"Are you ready for school this year?" he asked. He knew how bad his cousin wanted to go to the University of Miami with most of her high school buddies. She also wanted to get a better education, of course.

"Yeah, I'm ready."

"It's a dorm right?" Pablo probed, as he pulled into the parking lot of the college campus. It was filled with bad bitches.

"Yep, and I can't wait to get away from daddy! O.M.G.!"

"Why? He treats you good; the old man really spoils you." He parked and stepped out of his new fly car.

"I'm older now and I realize living under daddy will always hold me back from truly blossoming," she said, watching Pablo approach a beautiful woman.

"I'm Pablo."

"Hey, I'm Amora and I'm not interested in what you're trying to sell," the woman told him rudely.

"I'm just trying to build a friendship with you and get to know you, mami."

"I think you a little slow, papi. I'm gay," she lied.

"I like 'em gay." He smiled.

"Well, I was born a man." Amora walked off and Christina laughed so hard at Pablo's rejection.

They walked to the entrance of the school and went inside so she could purchase her books for classes.

Romell Tukes

CHAPTER 14

MIAMI BEACH, MIAMI

The next morning, Boss woke up to his little brother banging on his front door and his brother seemed to be in panic mode. At first, he was going to spazz out on him for ringing his doorbell so early.

"I knew it was that nigga, bro, who else send hitters in fuckin' ninja cloths to come kill a nigga?" Lil BD said, still heated over what had happened to him a few hours before he'd arrived to his brother's crib.

"This nigga been laying low for a while so why would he just pop back up on some wild man shit?" Boss replied with a confused look fixed on his face.

"Fuck all that, bro, my whole issue is why come at me? I'm chillin'." Lil BD had been complaining since he'd got there and Boss was sick of it because Lil BD knew he would eventually have to deal with that type of shit when you signed up for the streets.

"You knew what it was when you jumped off the porch," Boss told him. Lil BD gave him a nasty look.

"Yeah, but I got out to become a better person and to hopefully live my life in peace."

"Sometimes shit don't go as planned, bro. You know that," Boss reminded him, because the way he saw it, out of all people, Lil BD should've known that from first-hand experience.

"Them niggas almost had me, bro, now I gotta wear a slingshot over my arm." Lil BD lifted his arm up.

"You lucky"

"Nah, some bad bitch saved me, bro. I couldn't see her face but she was on fire—I could tell by her eyes." Lil BD thought about the women who had saved him from his casket.

"You ain't tell me that."

"I was too ashamed, but I'm telling you, bro, shawty had a team of shooters and they took out the OPPs like it was nothing," Lil BD boasted.

"What was her name?" Boss asked. "Did you catch it?" He allowed his mind to roam momentarily. "'Cause we don't got too many allies, especially not in Atlanta, bro," he added.

"Her name was Vina."

"What?" Boss' body froze at the mention of her name.

"Vina, nigga?" Lil BD saw Boss' reaction and started to wonder what was going on.

"She runs the Costa Rican Cartel but we never had any dealing with her so it's weird to me," Boss told him.

"I don't know, but I want them fools who tried to kill me, cuz."

"You out the game, right?"

"I don't know yet, bro, but I can't let this shit slide, bro. I feel like a bitch now and I was drunk, so them bitch ass niggas could've really fucked me over."

"Facts, but you here now, and tomorrow is the family meeting."

"So, what the fuck you tellin' me for? I'm not fuckin' with that lane—I already told you that," Lil BD stated, getting frustrated because he'd already been shot.

"They're gonna come back for yo' dumb ass then what?"

"I'ma be okay."

"Whatever, my nigga, but if I was you, I'd be smarter." Boss left Lil BD to himself to give him time to get his mind right.

St. Mark, FL

THE ISLAND OF ST. MARK was a village in Wakulla County near Tallahassee. Though it was a small village with less than 300 people residing, half of them were well-to-do rich people with drug habits. The Hara Family ran the small island, and many others like Saint Barthélemy, where they controlled the drugs.

Rowley and his crew got off the boat that had traveled from Key West, FL. It would be a big day for him because it was the day he would take over the city; however, the problem was trying to take the area from his wife's brother, someone he was cool with.

The man's name was Lil Hara and he was doing big things, but what Rowley knew for a fact was Lil Hara had been coping drugs from the Haitian Mafia for years, and he felt like it was time to speak up. He loved his wife to death but he had to take care of business, and it was nothing personal.

Five deep, with assault rifles and ready to make a move, they took a truck to Lil Hara's house. The ride was silent all the way there.

Within a few minutes, they made it to Lil Hara's crib and there were all types of luxury cars parked in the front of the driveway.

Rowley looked around for the security guards but there weren't any, which made it very easy for them to enter the crib.

The goons ambushed the front of the house with their weapons in-hand, ready to fuck some shit up. Out of all the rooms in the mansion, Rowley knew Lil Hara was downstairs doing his voodoo. The whole Hara family practiced voodoo, especially Rowley's wife and Lil Hara.

They walked down the stairs and when they reached the last step, they entered a dark room and there was incense burning. Lil Hara's dreads hung down to the floor—they were so long, when he stood up, they touched his feet.

Boc! Boc! Boc! Boc!—without hesitation, Rowley's friends shot into the back of Lil Hara's head. When his dead body collapsed on to the thick rugs, Rowley's goons raided the crib.

Romell Tukes

CHAPTER 15

MIAMI, FL ...

Lil BD exited Boss' crib which was located on the South Beach strip. He'd been at his brother's condo for a few days and he loved it. Being back in Miami, he felt like life couldn't get any better for him. Nevertheless, having to leave his home and being on the run because someone was trying to kill him, made him feel like a bitch.

Walking to his new Lambo SUV, he noticed a note on the window of his car. "What the fuck is this?" he said to himself, as his eyes scanned the paper and he began to read the short note:

I'm Vina, the woman who saved your life in Atlanta. I hope you remember. If not, then I'm sure soon your memory will be refreshed. Next Saturday, at 12 p.m., I want you to meet me at Disneyland in Orlando.

Lil BD put the note down as he reflected on the day he almost lost his life at hands of his enemy.

"Oh, the cartel bitch who saved your life," Boss started with a laugh.

"My nigga, please." Lil BD was still ashamed.

"Bro, you're still in the gang family so you don't have too many options ... this is your life," Boss said, being honest.

"I run my own life, but anyway, I'm 'bout to slide to the mall real quick." Lil BD ain't really wanna talk about it.

"Listen, just think about it," Boss told him, before hanging up.

Lil BD shook his head and thought about the meeting coming up even though he really didn't give a fuck.

NORTH MIAMI, FL

THE THOUGHT OF VINA'S SEXY, BEAUTIFUL FACE made him blush. Lil BD had never had someone save him so because Vina had been his amour and savior, he valued her, somewhat.

In a few days, his mom would be holding a meeting in Haiti. He'd been invited to attend but he wasn't sure what his plans were yet because he really wanted to fall back.

Getting inside the truck, he received a call from Boss and he put the call on speaker.

"Where are you at, boi?" Boss asked, as he sped down the highway. Lil BD could hear the wind in the background.

"Leaving your spot."

"You still coming out to Haiti with me?" Boss asked, after a short pause.

"I never said I was, nigga. What the fuck?" Lil BD didn't want to be around his mom or fake ass uncles.

"Think about it 'cause we need you right now."

"Fuck all dat!"

***

Luc went out to Miami really quick, just so he could check out one of his restaurants. Opening a few restaurants, he was focused on a legit chain of businesses in the islands, and, of course, the states,.

Pushing a Maybach threw the city, he felt like a king, so of course, he had to move like a boss through the streets.

The meeting with the family members would be happening soon. Luc had over 300 workers in Haiti who been pushing for him, and he would be having a meeting with his workers as well.

Stopping at the light, he hadn't peeped the van pulling up behind him, or the all-black one going towards him. Before he had realized what was about to take place it popped off.

Tat! Tat! Tat! Tat!–bullets ripped through the air and bounced off the car ripped through the car hitting everything in their paths, except Luc— he'd recently had the car bulletproofed for times like that.

He ran the red light and laughed when he saw the pink Lambo parked in the cut and Lexus sitting in the driver's seat smiling at him. He hated Lexus and her entire family so seeing the smirk on her face made his blood boil to the max, but tonight would be the night she signed her life away.

"Little bitch, " he mumble to himself. He pondered on whether or not he should tell Boss about the little event, but he knew Lexus was still Boss' wife.

Before they'd gotten married, he'd warned Boss about Miami bitches because they seemed to always be on some extra shit, especially the rich ones.

Luc focused his thoughts on the meeting that would take place in less than 24 hours, back home, in Haiti. He'd heard what had happened to his nephew, Lil BD, in Atlanta, but he couldn't respect Lil BD for turning on his family and walking away from the game.

Romell Tukes

CHAPTER 16

PATIO-VILLA, HAITI

Janella sat at the head of the table looking around. Everybody seated was somebody in the family and had a position with the Haitian Mafia.

"Look at my beautiful family," Janella said, showing her beautiful smile.

"Mom, come on with the bullshit you got a lot of games," Boss told her.

"Just trying to gas y'all up." Janella laughed. She could tell Luc wasn't in the most joyful of moods—as usual.

"Let's get this shit over with," Luc said, giving Boss and Lil BD a dirty look because of the recent shoot-out with Lexus.

He felt as though he couldn't trust a soul— family or friends because either would be the first to cross you.

"This nigga looking like he on one," Lil BD told Boss in his ear, as they took seats next to each other.

"He good." Boss wasn't stressed or really worried about Luc's funny style.

"As you all know, right now we all got a lot going on right now, and shit ain't going as planned with my ex-brother," Janella said sadly, because shit had been going all wrong.

"What's up with Louis bitch ass?" Lil BD asked. The last thing he remembered, Louis was on some sneak-shady shit trying to double cross whoever got in his way.

"Louis is dead meat," Luc said, and pulled out a cigar.

"I sent someone to New York to kill Louis but that shit backfired, and if I know my brother like I think I know him, he's out there right now, waiting in the cut somewhere," Janella said.

"All he gonna do is sneak attack us, "Boss stated.

"It's still an attack," Luc added.

"Louis a pussy," Lil BD said with a little smirk.

"Never underestimate your enemy or give them less than what they deserve. Trust me, that was my dad's downfall in his prime." Janella used to listen when her dad talked when she was a little girl, but back then she hadn't known anything about life or her family ties.

"Facts," Luc added, puffing on the cigar like a true boss.

"We still have the Dominicans and Trin's on our line, trying to find a lane in what we're building. Miami is ours, period. We took over the city and robbed it from the Cubans but we'll never let anybody run us out of our city," Janella added.

"We got another problem we slept on. "Luc looked at Boss while he spoke as if he'd had something to do with it.

"What is it?" Janella asked, already having enough on her plate.

"Lexus tried to kill me the other day while I was driving. but the bitch ain't know I had that bullet proof put on my car." Luc winked at Boss.

"No wonder he's moving funny," Lil BD stated.

"I hope you don't think I had anything to do with that shit?" Boss blurted out.

'Nah, if I did, you would be dead already," Luc told him.

"I'm sure."

"She may still mad about her father. Y'all did kill him," Janella said to Luc.

"I'ma kill her slowly." Luc's words were slow and painful.

"Call me 'cause I wanna watch," Boss stated being funny.

"We got a bigger problems right now, boys ... like your ex-wife, Kamla," Janella said, speaking of her number one rival.

"I'ma try to reach out," Luc said

"Sounds like some shady shit going on somewhere in those lines," Lil BD told Luc, trying to test his loyalty.

"What, little nigga?" Luc spit. He had taken Lil BD's words to heart.

"Relax! Y'all act like bitches, but we need to figure this shit out soon. The product is still on ten and all the customers are loving us, but I wanna lower the price. I was thinking we do that in a few days," she spoke to Luc

"You sure, sis?"

"Yes."

"That's smart, Ma," Lil BD stated, knowing she would lock the game down.

"You back in the family?" she asked her youngest son.

"I'm thinking about it, but most likely I'm back for good," Lil BD told them all. He'd been thinking about it for a few days now and he was ready.

"Welcome back," his mom told him.

"Let Boss update you on what's been going on since I'm sure he knew." Luc rolled his eyes at Boss because he felt as if Boss wasn't trustworthy.

"You're going hard today, goofy," Boss said.

"I have to go back. I want you all to keep your focus on Chloe, Danilo, Pablo, Lexus, and especially Kamala." When she said Luc's ex-wife's name, she gave him a real sturdy look.

"I'm reaching out like I told you but it's Rowley. I know it is." Luc tried to defend Kamla.

"Fuck all of them," Boss said.

"All of you call me in a few days, In the meantime, security is here for you whenever you need them," she said. None of them liked using the guards who got paid to protect them.

"Fuck security! We mobbin'," Boss added, as they ended the meeting.

Romell Tukes

CHAPTER 17
ORLANDO, FL

Lil BD and Boss parked in the parking lot of the Disneyland Amusement Park, to meet Vina. The lot had cars parked in lines all over the place, every day. People from all over came out to enjoy themselves at the best park ever.

"How are you gonna find her?" Boss grabbed his gun and asked, as he exited the car.

"I got it, bro, "Lil BD said, taking a deep breath.

"A'ight, let's go."

"Huh?" Lil BD looked at him as if he had lost his mind.

"Nigga, we out! She's waiting and I hope that bitch not dumb enough to pull a move in public 'cause I ain't killed a nigga in broad daylight in a while," Boss stated.

"Stay here, bro, I'ma handle this shit real quick."

"Are you sure? 'Cause you don't even know the bitch," Boss added

"I'm straight. I don't feel them types of vibes from her at all, bro, and if that was the case, she had her chance to kill me," Lil BD made a clear point.

"I'ma sit here then, but if you see any funny shit, let me know."

"Nigga, if I see any movement I'm bustin' first, bro." Lil BD got out of the car and made his way to the entrance. The only thing on his mind was how he would know who she was. He didn't have her number nor did he know what she looked like since he'd only seen her eyes. But never could he forget the person who had saved his life.

Walking around, he went toward the food court area, hoping to find the beautiful woman.

Vina sat patiently at the food court, eating a salad while waiting to see her guest. She knew a public place like this would be her best bet to ensure both parties felt relaxed and comfortable.

She had houses in Orlando and Miami that she rarely frequented, so coming out to the states was very much needed; besides, she was on a mission.

Looking around, she saw Lil BD coming her way but he looked lost, so she stood up to help him.

When she waved him down, he looked in her direction and a confused expression spread across his face. He had no clue she was *that* sexy and he'd spotted her the moment he'd entered. Unfortunately, he'd mistook her for a stuck-up model-type bitch.

"Hey BD," Vina said and displayed a welcoming smile.

"How are you doing?" Lil BD tried to play it cool but her beauty was on another level.

"Thanks for coming out."

"You saved my life so I'm forever in your favor," he told her.

"It's cool. It was personal, Lil BD, trust me," she told him.

"Who was that anyway?" He asked the question that had been on his mind evet since the home vision.

"Maloney's people came for you. I got an alert that morning from my people in Atlanta and they warned me that he was looking for someone close to the Haitian Mafia," she stated before sipping from a glass of orange juice.

"Maloney? How the fuck he find me? I knew it was him," he replied, as if a light bulb had suddenly gone off over his head.

"I don't know but I'm on his ass. He did a lot of shit he wasn't supposed to do," she said.

"I bet," he said frowning, "niggas like him can't be trusted one bit. Facts."

"Agree."

"You came out here alone?" Lil BD asked.

"No, but I know Boss is parked in the lot," she confirmed.

"How do you know?" he asked.

She laughed. "I have people all over this place, BD. I'm always on point because I have a lot of haters," she told him.

"Join the club."

"I haven't been in this game too long but what I do know is, your family is very smart and they're well-respected in my eyes." She spoke strongly of his family.

"We stand strong."

"I see, but I got a whole cartel family to run myself."

"So I heard, but you look so young."

"I am, BD, but I have to do what I have to do. If I don't, my people will starve and have nothing at all." She loved her people and her country.

"I feel you, and I know that can be a lot of pressure."

"It is … you have no idea how much, but I know it's for the right reason."

"Facts. My people know of you."

"I wanna do business with your family, BD. I believe we can help each other out," she told him.

"Maybe. But that's something I would have to speak with my mom about," he told her.

"Okay, that's fine."

"I already told her and I tried to go ahead and set up a meeting." Lil BD looked at how sexy she was and wanted to get to know her a little better, but he had a feeling it was bad timing.

"Thanks." She stood up to leave and handed him a piece of paper. Lil BD looked at her hips and ass as she walked away looking like a Coke Cola bottle.

Romell Tukes

CHAPTER 18
NORTH MIAMI, FL

Pablo waited at a smoothie shop for Amore to arrive. He had finally gotten her to come out and spend a few minutes with him. The life-style he lived made it really hard to enjoy the finer things in life but he never complained about the game that had chosen him.

He rocked an all-white Amiri top and bottom, with shoes to match, and he was looking real flyy. Pablo saw Amore getting out of her car, and she was wearing leggings and a Louis Vuitton top, and holding a matching purse.

There was something special about Amore and he wanted to be the one to find out but she was a different type.

"Hey," Amore said, as she placed her bag on the table and sat down.

"Thanks for coming out. You look nice." He complimented her and tried to butter her up.

"I just came from the gym so stop lying shit face," she joked.

"Oh well, at least you came out of the gym looking like a snack. You like smoothies and shit?" he asked.

"Yes, I love them, especially after a workout. OMG, you don't know!" she boosted looking at the menu.

"That's what's up, ma, but tell me about yourself."

"I mean, what do you wanna know? Shit, I'm me," she shot back.

"Okay, first, how was your childhood and growing up?" he asked, sounding interested, but he was really trying to get to know her in and out.

"I mean, shit, growing up in New York I was like any other kid. What else do you want me to say?"

"You got brothers or sisters?" Pablo asked her, trying to get her full attention.

"Yeah, I got a big family, papi, and believe me, we are all crazy." She giggled.

"Ain't we all, but how's school going? I like that you stay focused 'cause every time I call you, you studying or doing something else dealing with school."

"Yep, I love college. I be so focused on trying to make a living for my future because you need a degree for everything nowadays—even to work in McDonald's," she told him.

"You right, but you gotta stay focused and do what you have to do so you can succeed in life, because it's hard out here."

"True dat, but what do you do for a living?" She'd never gotten the chance to ask him but she had an idea what he did judging by his swag and the way he moved.

"I'm a contractor."

"For what?"

"I take contracts on a lot of new businesses that opened up here in North Miami— like hotels and restaurants," Pablo said, coming up with a smooth lie, but he could tell she wasn't buying it at all.

"That's good but what are your future plans?"

"Me?"

"No, your twin dummy." She joked.

"I wanna be a billionaire," he told her, being honest.

"First, you gotta become a millionaire," she told him.

"Facts, but I might already be there." He played with her because he'd been a millionaire ever since he was a teen.

"Right, and I'm Brittany Spears." She laughed as they ordered their smoothies and enjoyed their day.

TEXAS

Chloe came out to Austin, TX to speak with a man named Jess. Jess ran a Mexican Cartel in Mexico but he controlled a large drug supply from New York to Cali.

"Jess, good to meet you. I've heard a lot about you," Chloe said, as she took a seat and joined Jess for a business dinner at his mansion.

"Well Chloe, I would say it's nice to meet you too, but I've heard a lot of bad things about you." Jess was a handsome killer with one of the most powerful Mexican Cartel army's.

"Don't believe everything you hear these days, trust me, I never crossed a soul unless they crossed me," she replied in the soft tone.

"I can respect that, somewhat."

"These days, and for many reasons, I don't trust people, but I've always admired the way you handle business." Chloe tried to gas him up to only get a laugh.

"Why are you here, Chloe? How can I help you?"

"Okay, I'm just gonna put it all out there … I need your help, and I think we can do good business together, Jess."

"I work better alone, Chloe, and to keep it real, you bring too much drama and heat to people's business— if I can speak the truth with all due respect," he said, hoping she would get up and leave.

"Before you say no, I'm going to tell you who I'm at war with." I don't care," Jess shot back.

"The man who killed your brother is who I'm at war with," she said, before getting up to leave. As Jess thought about the man, Luc, who killed his brother years ago, his mind wondered.

Romell Tukes

CHAPTER 19

Key West, FL

Luc made his way to the large yacht for his lunch date with one of his most dangerous rivals. Since the family meeting, she'd been trying to put some plans together.

The longer his family was at war with people and other families, the more he lost, so he had to come up with a plan. Luc came to an understanding within himself that Kamla was still legally his wife and would listen at times.

Calling Kamla was hard but he had to do it, not only for his family's business, but there was still a lot of shit between them, and today he hoped to put it all out on the table.

Walking onto the boat, he saw her sitting alone on the lower deck with her back turned, drinking from a glass of wine.

"Hey, wife," Luc said, approaching her from behind. There were no guards insight which was odd because she rolled deep. Nonetheless, he did peep the AR-15 assault rifle next to her foot.

"Deadbeat husband, how've you been?" she mocked him.

Luc laughed and sat down. He couldn't help but notice how good she looked in the Versace dress and her beautiful hair was draped across her shoulders.

"Thanks again for coming out, but I really needed to express myself and get this shit off my chest."

"You're quick to say how you feel but you don't give two fucks about the next person's feelings and that says a lot about who you truly are." Luc made eye contact with her just so she would know how serious he was. "Kamla, you've never expressed shit to me since I've known you."

"You never let me," she shot back.

"Okay, maybe I'm wrong but that's why I'm here."

"No, you're here on business trying to make a deal or come to some type of understanding, or better yet, you're here for an argument." She smiled as the words left her mouth because the moment Luc had walked on the boat, she could read his mind by his facial expression.

"So, you know me?"

"I do know you, Luc. And one thing I do know is you or your sister can't ever be trusted," she replied, looking into the nice, clear water.

"To this day, I've never crossed you or nobody else I fuck with. So let's be real, Kamla. How many times have you plotted to kill me?" he asked.

"Many times, and I'm actually trying to kill you now. The only reason I didn't have a hundred niggas here waiting on you is because I wanted to at least give you a proper farewell," she said. "Face it, one of us has to go."

"Like that?"

"Yes, y'all killed my brother and my father so this shit will never end, bitch."

"Okay, I tried."

"Yep, but not hard enough."

"I tried too, Kamla, and we need to stop this shit before it gets worse."

"I'm ready."

"Get ready," she stated, before standing from her seat, so she could escort him outside.

"Okay, Kamla, but just know I really hate to be the one to do this."

"Hahahaa! Luc, get your mind right, playa. You fuckin' with a killer boss bitch," she stated.

"I hear you," Luc stated then turned to walk off the boat.

"I hope you do!" she said, as she watched him leave.

PALM BEACH COUNTY, FL

RUSH AND A FEW OF HIS GOONS sat at the round table looking at all the stacks of money.

"This is the life we all have in a store if shit goes right, but loyalty is a must," Rush stated.

"Facts, dawgs," Appeal stated, seriously. He was ready to get money with his big homie and childhood friend.

78

"We're going to war with Big Hulu and I got the drop on where his baby's mother lives." Rush had received a call from his crip homie.

"We got a big problem, bro. Fat Jack just got killed coming out of the precinct a few minutes ago," Gotti said.

"Fat Jack?"

"Yeah, cuz."

"Them Spanish niggas did it," Rush said, already knowing it had been the Opps.

"What the fuck was Fat Jack doing coming out the police station, cuz?" Three Dub shouted. He'd overheard the whole conversation because the phone had been on speaker.

"That's trill, bro. Why was she even over there?" Rush questioned.

"That's a good question, dawg, because baby girl was acting funny, real talk, cuz. But I'ma look into it. My uncle's a cop over there," Gotti said, before hanging up.

"This shit 'bout to get real ugly tonight, bro. Load up two trucks and slide on all them niggas, bro," Rush told his most trusted goons.

Rush had been going at it with Big Hulu's people for years because of the turf war and the hate they had for one another. In a few days he'd need more work, so he'd have to hit up Chloe or Hitler but he really hated Hitler's energy.

"I'm on it, bro." Three Dub got up from the table and began to make calls to his little shooters.

Later that night, the city raised the murder rate when seven people were killed and four were injured in two massive shootouts.

Romell Tukes

CHAPTER 20
NORTH MIAMI, FL

Amora looked amazing in her dress and heels and she felt special when Pablo took her on another at a restaurant near the Blu Fountain hotels which cost a handful.

"You sure know how to cater to a woman," she said, while eating a fancy meal. She couldn't tell you what it was.

"I just know how to be a gentleman and treat my women." "Pablo needed a woman like Amora in his life, to balance it out, because at times, life for him was crazy.

"I see but this could going further but we need to make some promises," she told him.

"What type of promises?" he asked, with a funny look on his face since he wasn't yet ready to commit.

"I'm too bossy to be fuckin' with you and I want this to be right for the both of us."

"So, you my girl now?"

"I'm not saying that, but what I will tell you is that I'm feeling you a lot, and I'm ready to start a relationship if it's real."

"Are you sure?" he asked.

"Yeah, dummy." She chuckled.

"What's the promise because I don't sell my soul to the devil"

"Well, I'm not the devil. I'm the grim reaper," she joked.

"I can tell, but you know the life I live so are you sure this is what you really want?"

"Yes, trust me, you're special"

"I'm feeling you too, but what's the big promise?"

"Never cross me," she told him, sounding like a big-time mob boss.

"You sound like me."

"Word." Amore looked around at the amazing hotel.

"I'll never cross you, mami. I'm just gone off your energy"

"As long as we got this under control,'" she added.

"So, where we go from here?" he asked.

"I'm all yours." She kissed him softly, happy for their new love.

"So, I'm happy to be yours"

"Me too." She couldn't stop smiling at him.

"Let's go finish the night off," he stated.

"I'm down for that," she said. She stood up and prepared to leave, and she was ready for a new start at love.

DOWNTOWN MIAMI

MALONEY CAME OUT TO SEE a few dancers at a club he'd heard of a while back but had never been to. Many things had happened since he'd been in Miami looking for Luc and Boss.

Things hadn't been the same with him since he'd been beefing with Vina. He felt a little awkward even though he had his goons on deck ready for whatever.

"Hi, papi, how's your night going?" a sexy, Spanish woman asked.

"I'm good."

"I can give you the best time of your life tonight."

"Well, I'm new to the city and I would like to experience something new and very different," he told her, as she moved in between his knees, in the private VIP section.

"You know a man named Boss?" Maloney asked, stopping her.

"No," she replied.

"Luc?"

"Luc the Haitian guy?"

"Yeah, he's tall and dark skinned with dreads."

"He comes through every once and a while," the dancer said, dancing to the beat.

"I need you to go find him and set him up."
"How much?" she asked.

"What do you mean, *how much*?" Maloney repeated over the loud music, as the women continued to dance on him.

"I need money, boo. I'm sorry … ain't shit free in life," she stated seriously.

"Okay, you have to send me your cash app info," he stated reluctantly.

"I'm sending it to you tonight," she told him, before getting up to leave.

SOUTH MIAMI, FL

BOSS HAD TO MEET SPIKE in Chicago but he needed to chat with Lil BD before leaving, so they went out to a cigar shop to chat.

"You watch sports?" Lil BD asked, looking up toward the TV at a college basketball game.

"I'm too busy for sports."

"I hear you, but I forgot to tell you Luc hollered at me."

"Oh yeah? 'Bout what?" Boss asked, since he knew how the two of them felt about one another.

"About Louis, but to be real, I really don't trust that nigga, Luc," Lil BD said.

"He's family, my brother, and he's on our side until he's shows us different," Boss said.

"I guess,"

"You gotta be thicker in this game, bro."

"I know," Lil BD shout back

"Never go off your emotions 'cause that'll get a nigga killed quick these days. And don't let your feelings persuade your mental, bro, 'cause that's the fasted way to crash, and not only will you wreck yourself, but you'll wreck me also," Boss schooled him. He knew his little brother could be stubborn at times, so he always tried to make him see the bigger picture in life and business.

"You right, folk." Lil BD nodded his head even though he wasn't really trying to hear what Boss was saying.

"What's up with that cartel bitch?" Boss asked

"She cool, bro. We talk daily and build on real shit and she really trying to fuck with us."

"We don't even know her, bro, so you should take it slow on her," Boss suggested.

"I know. I'm just feeling her out and I think she's official, bro."

"Nigga, you just met the bitch, so how the fuck you think she official?" Boss knew his little brother could easily get caught up in a bitch, like a spider in a web.

"Trust me, bro, I feel it."

Boss looked at Lil BD as if he'd lost his mind. "Lil BD, just because you got a good feeling about a bitch, don't mean she got good intentions toward you."

"Trust me my nigga she can elevate our shit"

"Maybe, but this shit is bigger than us my guy. Mommy and Luc ain't goin' for that shit, bro, and you know that.

"It's worth a try, right?" Lil BD knew Boss was right but he didn't want to show his hand.

"You fuck her?"

"Nah."

"Nigga, you lying," Boss said, hoping Lil BD hadn't wilded out like that, because Vina could be an enemy or a snake in the grass.

"Bro, I know how to control myself,"

"Shit, nigga, I know you."

"Okay, you right, folk, but I'm focusing, bro, trust me. Since I'm back, I put myself first and mind my own business. It's hard to even trust people, bro. Anyway, I told you to never just open the doors like that for a bitch 'cause the moment she give you some pussy, bro, that shit goes out the window.

"Okay, now maybe that bro, "Lil BD laughed.

"I know." Boss knew Lil BD was smart and knew how to think and move when it came to situations like that, so he changed subjects.

CHAPTER 21
SOUTH BEACH, MIAMI

Luc's driver parked in front of the Caribbean restaurant that sat in the center of South Beach Blvd near the action. The restaurant sold the best island foods, drinks, and smoothies in Miami, and it was a five-star rating.

Opening the restaurant in Miami was not a plan for Luc until Boss put the idea in his head. Boss explained to him that there was a lot of Haitians who had been in America so long, they'd forgot what Haitian food tasted like.

After doing some thinking, Luc took it upon himself to open the restaurant, and now it was a big success overall, thanks to Boss pushing the idea. Soon, Luc thought about opening another spot in New York, LA, Chicago and ATL—the hottest cities in the states.

Getting out of the Rolls Royce truck, he stretched his arm. He loved the city's hot summers, and of course, looking at the beautiful women. But Luc had a different type of standard for women these days and nobody could top it except Kamla, but she was on a different level—at least, mentally.

Luc's restaurant manager was inside moving chairs around with the employees before opening in ten minutes.

"Aye, boss man, I ain't know you were coming," Carlos, a Haitian man, said, stopping to shake his boss' hand.

"I was in town so I figured I'd stop by," Luc said.

"I have everything in the safe inside the back office. Do you wanna go check with me?" Carlos asked. A customer walked in but the restaurant was still closed.

"Sure," Luc said. He was getting ready to follow Carlos to the back but something told him to turn around.

"Sir, we're closed," Carlos yelled to the man wearing all-black

"Bonjour," the customer said, before he pulled out a gun and shot Carlos in the face.

Luc took cover just as he recognized the shooter's face. Louis.

Tat! Tat-Tat! Tat!

Luc got low and went for his weapon and fired back at his own brother. When he hit one of the employees in the face, the man dropped in the doorway.

"I'm kill you Va te faite foutre arifor!" Louis yelled, calling Luc a bitch-ass nigga while cursing him out in their language.

Luc shouted out how he was gonna kill him before letting off a few rounds, glazing Louis in his side, but his gun jammed.

Tat! Tat! Tat! Tat!

Louis saw Luc had a gun problem so he took advantage and tried to air him out, closing in on him, but Luc jumped up and shot out the back.

Luc made it out of the back, leaving Louis behind as he went through an alley making his way to the main street.

Looking for his driver, he saw him laid out on the floor bleeding to death, as civilians surrounded him and tried to save his life in front of the Rolls Royce SUV.

Luc walked off smoothly once he saw Louis was nowhere in sight, but he was upset he'd almost let his brother kill him.

MIAMI, FL

CHRISTINA WAS IN SCHOOL going to her locker to prepare for her next class which was science, her least favorite.

"Christina!" A female voice yelled out from the left of her.

Looking through the crowd she saw Amora approaching him with a smile while waving her down. Last week, she'd seen Pablo and Amora talking and looking really happy together, so when she asked Pablo about his relationship with Amora. When Pablo told her the two were a couple, she wasn't shocked because she'd caught the energy they shared the first day of school when he first saw Amora in the lot.

"Hey, Amora," Christina said, smiling.

"What you doing?"

"Getting ready for my next class in the science building."

"Oh, great. I'm walking that way anyway so how are your grades coming along?" Amora asked, genuinely.

"I can do better in math but I just have to get more into my books," Christian stated seriously, as she made her way through the packed hallways.

"Facts, but I can help?"

"I'm okay, but if I need help, I'll be sure to let you know."

"Great."

"How are things with you and Pablo?" Christina asked nosily.

"Me and babe good. He's a really good guy."

"He is?" Christina thought she was bugging because Amora didn't know about Pablo's lifestyle.

"I'm so happy."

"That's great." Christina and Amora walked off and headed to their classes and continued to talk about Pablo and life.

Romell Tukes

CHAPTER 22
OAXACA, MEXICO

Jess sat in one of many mansions. He watch through the window as his horses ran around in his backyard, just as they did every morning before his workers fed and trained them.

As child growing up in Mexico, he'd loved horses and land. There was something about land and having animals that made life seem so special.

Lately, dealing with Chloe felt a little awkward, but he also had his reasons for entering the snake pit with a vicious king cobra like Chloe.

Jess had a meeting to attend in London the upcoming weekend with a few other drug families from the UK and London areas. A few years back, he'd put a lot of time and money into building a foundation out there. Working with the European country made him a richer man and open to new ideas in life that he was now proud of.

"Jess," an older woman said. She rushed over to him with blood on her hands and tears in her eyes.

"What happened?" Jess panicked. He'd never seen the look of death on the maid's face before and she looked as if she'd seen a ghost..

"Someone killed Jasper," she cried out.

"My nephew?" he shouted. He rushed out of the room to the upper level where his nephew slept and played.

Jess had been taking care of his nephew since he was a little baby because his mother, who was also Jess' blood sister, had allowed drugs to take her out at an early age.

Standing in the doorway of the room, Jess saw a small note on the floor. He picked it up and rushed inside to see his little nephew's throat cut open with large stab wounds to his little body.

"Nooo, papi, not you!" Jess mourned and cried out loud.

After several minutes of crying and trying to control his emotions, he finally read the letter:

This is a warning sign. You chose to fuck with the wrong person and doing so cost you dearly. There will be more to come, trust us.

Jess had tears in his eyes and it was the first time he'd cried in a long time. He knew deep down inside, the Haitian Mafia were the ones to blame because he knew how they operated, and killing people and family members had always been their modus operandi, or their M.O., if you will. If he knew who had actually been behind little Jasper's gruesome killing, he would be shocked.

Tortuga Island, Haiti

FLYING OUT TO HAITI, VINA WAS ON HER PRIVATE JET ALONE. She looked out and stared into the clouds, lost in her thoughts.

Lil BD had set up a meeting with his mom and Vina which would take place once she landed. At first, she had been unsure about going out there for a meeting but she knew it would be beneficial.

Things between her and Lil BD were going so well and they were building a real bond. For some reason, the connection she shared with him was one of a kind and she loved it.

Nowadays, finding a good vibe with a person was hard to do because everybody was out for self. The feeling Lil BD gave her not only made her feel special, but it made her feel as if she was the only woman on earth, and she loved that feeling.

***

Vina's private jet landed in a long strip on what seemed like the hottest day of the year. Getting off the jet she saw how beautiful the city was and how much she liked the island. She peered over at the black SUV that was parked by another jet, over where Lil BD stood. She couldn't help but be full of smiles at the sight of him. Every time she saw him her stomach would flutter from the butterflies and happiness would overcome any negative thoughts she'd had.

"I see you always on time," Vina started, once she'd made her way over to her beau.

"I'm always on time for a Queen like yourself." Lil BD flattered her and bent to give her a warm embrace.

"You smell so good." She inhaled his designer cologne.

"Thanks, but you ready for tonight?" he asked. He picked her bags up and placed them inside the back.

"More ready than I'll ever be, I guess, but I think it will go well. I heard a lot of great things about your family," Vina stated.

"You heard anything from Maloney yet?"

"He's somewhere in Miami but I figured you all would be able to get to him before I do," she replied.

"I know he's in hiding."

"That's what he does." She sat close to Lil BD as they talked and made their way to Janella's house on the island.

The ten minute ride was the longest ten minutes of Vina's life as they arrived at the big mansion on the small island.

"Wow! This is nice," she said, as she entered the glass double doors which were surrounded by guards, and the smell of good Caribbean food could be smelled in the air.

Lil BD saw his mom coming down the stairs in an all-white Chanel dress looking like an angel fresh out of hell.

"Nice to meet you, Vina," Janella said, as she shook Vina's hand.

"Likewise, Mrs. Janella. I've heard so much about you," Vina told her. She gazed momentarily, admiring how pretty Janella was.

"Follow me ... I want to speak with you one-on-one," Janella advised Vina. Lil BD had gone upstairs to get dressed and ready for dinner. Luc and Boss both were on their way from Miami so they would also be joining Janella for dinner.

Vina and Janella talked for an entire hour before dinner and they had begun looking into business plans for the future.

Romell Tukes

CHAPTER 23
WEST MIAMI, FL

Hitler had just dropped off Chloe after taking her to get her eyebrows done, like most females, it was something she did weekly along with getting her nails and hair done.

He was ready to help her send out the product to Alabama, Atlanta, and Palm Beach, but there had been something off about her. However, he had never been the type to press a bitch about nothing—nothing at all. To some point, he felt like their love life was more so business than anything. Though he didn't mind, he carried a lot of doubt in his heart about Chloe.

Not eating all day had his stomach hurting, so when he spotted the Pollo Tropical fast-food spot on his right, he pulled over to grab a bite to eat. Listening to YFN Lucci's first album, he pulled the vehicle into the parking lot.

Living in Miami felt like he'd finally made it but having to ride around with a gun at all times made it feel so much like Chicago. When he hopped out of the car, he was unaware of the Lambo pulling in after him. Hitler made his way to the entrance, and because niggas were constantly stealing, he looked to his left to check on his car.

As he looked at his car, he saw Lil BD jump out of a Lambo with the biggest assault rifle he'd ever seen in his life.

Hitler took off running into the fast-food restaurant and in his haste he pushed over two women while trying to save his own life.

Tat! Tat! Tat! Tat! Two young, black men standing next to the window got hit in the face by stray bullets.

Hitler ran through the other exit door and went across the street to a safe location. He watched Lil BD fire round after round toward him but he made it.

***

After the shootout, Lil BD got back in the Lambo and raced off, but he'd come so close to taking out his OPP.

He was on his way to the luxury Intercontinental Miami hotel to meet up with Vina since she'd asked him to pull up on such a beautiful morning.

Driving past Wendy's, he'd seen Hitler at the light waiting to make a left, so he tailed him. Seeing his ex-best friendstabbed his heart with a nail and he felt so good for trying to kill him. Driving to the hotel, he came up with another idea on how to get closer on him next time.

It took twenty minutes to arrive at Vina's hotel which was so high up, after parking in the front, he couldn't even see where it stopped when he got out of his car.

The hotel was classy and fancy as he walked through the front lobby to the elevators. On the ride up to the penthouse, he thought about what Vina might want but he didn't stress it.

The door it flew open and Vina was wearing a YSL silk robe and jumped in his arms as soon she laid her eyes on him. Lil BD was caught off guard as he stepped inside and that's when shit got crazy.

With no words from either of them, hurriedly, they took off each other's clothes. He carried her to the nearest bed, which just happened to be in the master bedroom. Lil BD wasted no time as he crawled between her sex legs and gave her pussy a gentle lick then began slowly sliding his tongue in and out of her hole, softly savoring her sweet, pretty kitty.

"Shit, uhmm…," she moaned, as she watched him get to work down south.

Lil BD ate the pussy so good; she came twice causing her body to shake while taking deep breaths.

"Fuck me," Vina said, in her soft tone.

Lil Bd followed her orders and slowly slid his manhood into her tiny pussy—she was tight and wet and her sex box contracted and gripped his cock like a glove.

He went deeper inside of her pussy and loved how she felt. Vina took inch by inch as she squirmed her hips into him.

"Ohhh fuck," she screamed, because she couldn't keep herself from yelling.

Her sexual roars only motivated Lil BD and made him pound even harder on her pussy. After the first nut, he turned her over and fucked her so good, she couldn't even see straight. They made love on the floor, in the kitchen, on the counter, the balcony, and the bathroom, until they both tapped out from having such rough sex.

All night they talked, made love, and close and personal with each other, building an even closer bond.

Romell Tukes

CHAPTER 24
SOUTH, MIAMI

K-Do and his baby mother had both gone out to Miami so they could meet up with someone for Kamla. The meeting was in regard to a big business move that involved sneaking drugs into the city of Miami.

"Where the fuck is this shit at?" K-Do asked. Sick of driving the rental car through Miami, he wanted to go back home to the island, but couldn't due to two upcoming meetings they had to attend.

"Bitch, just drive," K-Do said coldly as he puffed on a blunt. He'd flown out on the private jet with them and he loved traveling, especially on business trips, and he enjoyed taking care of the family funds because Kamla was always bossy.

"Okay, sorry, " his baby's mother replied.

"Drive to Port Blvd so we can get this shit taken care of." K-Do hated spending a whole day with his girl but at times she was good company.

"Okay, I gotta take this left on the Biscayne Blvd and take a turn on G Port of Miami, right?" she asked.

"Yeah, that's what the GPS says, right? You dumb ass bitch," K-Do shouted, as they made it to the part of Miami they'd been looking for. Today, he'd dressed casually wearing a nice bossy suit with a tie, and dress shoes to finish off his classy look.

K-Do grew up in Atlanta before moving back to the islands to get money, and he didn't have to look far because Kamla was his family and she had shit on lock.

There was no way he could go back to Trinidad without having the deal locked and sealed, and he needed to do the same thing with another deal that would take place the following day.

"You want me to wait right here for you, babe?" the beautiful, slim, golden-complexioned woman asked.

"Stay here 'cause this gonna be quick," K-Do told her as he climbed out of the car.

"Okay."

He walked around like a lost soul looking for a man named Matt, a White guy Kamla had spoken with the day before, on a third party call with him. There was a tall White man wearing an all-white outfit watching cargo come in and out.

"Sir, excuse me." K-Do approached the man from behind.

"Yes, how may I help you, sir?" the White man replied, looking K-Do up and down in his expensive suit.

"I'm looking for a guy name Matt."

"Who are you?"

"K-Do."

"Okay, we spoke earlier with Kamla, correct?" Matt asked to make sure K-Do was the right guy.

"Yeah, that's me."

"Good, follow me to my office. People always listen out here." Matt walked off and over to a trailer.

Once inside the trailer, they sat down and gave each other a cold stare, each one trying to read the other's body language.

"We believe you can be a big help to our family business," K-Do explained.

"Maybe, but I just need to know if I can trust you?" Matt asked.

"Trust is something my family stands on. We don't do bad business and we don't cross others in the game."

"I can understand that but trust is something that has to be earned not given," Matt spit game back.

"That's true, but sometimes you gotta take risks and do the best thing for the business," K-Do told him, looking at Matt's family photos on his desk.

"All money ain't good money."

"You like to buy your kids shit don't you?"

"Of course. They're in high school and college," Matt said still since he was still paying college fees for two of his kids.

Matt thought about what he was saying, and at the moment, he was late on bills and on the kids' school fees, so it was a bad time for him.

"Think about the kids," K-Do said, in an effort to persuade him.

"How much a month to bring your cargo in? What's in it, and how many times a month do I need to have my people on it, because Miami PD has been on us," Matt said, falling for the deal.

"Twice a month, drugs will be in them all, and it'll be coming from Trinidad."

"Okay, so now how much will I be paid?"

"Fifty off the top."

"What?" Matt shouted hoping he didn't mean a measly fifty dollars. He knew from experience most niggas would try to run game and use the cargo to ship drugs, sex slaves, or even guns and bombs. This was Matt's side-hustle and it had been going smoothly for twenty years while dealing with the cartels.

"Fifty thousand in cash."

"Oh, I see," he said, as dollar signs danced in his head, "that's a lot of money ... so I'll receive that once a month, correct?"

"Yeah, unless you fuck up then you done," K-Do stated.

"I won't, I swear, man, you and your people have my word and loyalty." Matt's face was very serious when he said that.

"Today we officially start."

"Good, what time and what's the number and barcode on the cargo?"

"5-9-1 and the barcode is 7-A-7-1-2-9-Z-I-M," K-Do read it off a piece of paper.

"I'll have it all prepared but when do I get paid?" Matt wanted to know.

"Soon. I'll cash app you the money or drop it off at your house." K-Do saw Matt's face frown.

"My house?"

"You think we don't know you live in Coconut Grove with three kids, and a wife who works as a nurse at Jackson Memorial Hospital?" K-Do shocked the hell out of Matt when he recited all of his personal info.

"Look, man, I won't ever screw you over."

"Trust me, I know."

"I'll be waiting for a drop," Matt told him, before K-Do left.

K-Do smiled thinking about how happy Kamla would be and how he was about to make over thirty thousand dollars every month because Kamla was offering Matt eighty thousand a month to deliver the drugs.

"It went good?" K-Do girl asked.

"Mind your business. We got another meeting tomorrow," K-Do told her, as she pulled off. Neither was aware they were being followed.

CHAPTER 25
PORT OF MIAMI, MIAMI
THE NEXT DAY ...

K-Do spoke with the co-director of the Port of Miami, the dock area where cargo was shipped out, from all over the world.

"I'll need to hold the cargo here for twenty-four hours every end of the month. My workers will arrive to pick up the canned goods," K-Do told the older White man walking past the forklifts and workers.

"I may have a spot for you, but if you don't mind me asking, where is your product being shopped to?"

"Texas, Arizona, and Ohio, sir," K-Do lied.

"Okay, have your people fax me all the info and I'll be able to handle everything for you." The White man shook hands with K-Do and confirmed the business arrangements.

Kamla sent K-Do out to Miami so he could use his business front where canned goods were sold. Using his front would get them a space on the dock so they could get drugs sent to the states. From there, they would be shipped to Brooklyn, NY, Philly, and New Jersey, and they already had family in place to move the weight for them.

Now that the deal was confirmed, K-Do had plans to go back to the hotel with his bodyguard. Keith's baby's mother awaited him at the hotel so they could rest before going back home. His baby's mother was from Brooklyn, NY, but she had a little West Indian in her blood. On his way to the SUV that had been parked across the street from the harbor, he called Kamla.

"Everything is solid," K-Do said.

"Great, so when can we start preparing?" Kamla sounded very happy.

"At the end of the month."

"This is a blessing, brotha. For months, I've been trying to make this happen. Thank you so much."

"No worries."

"When you come back we shall throw you a party," Kamla said.

"Oh no, me and Bri been out here partying for too long. We just wanna sleep and be with the kids," K-Do said, knowing how much Kamla disliked even hearing Bri's name.

"Why do you bring her with you on a business trips, K-Do?" Kamla's voice turned angry.

"She wanted to get away."

"*Get away*? How the fuck— You know what? I'll just see you when you get back,"Kamla said, before hanging up in his ear. K-Do looked at the phone and shook his head before climbing in the truck. *She's so immature and petty,* he thought about Kamla.

Kamla disliked Bri because she thought everything about her screamed gold digger. In Kamla's mind, all Bri wanted to do was lock her cousin down with kids and get her body done every other month.

K-Do drove to a fancy hotel so he could pack up, rest, and catch a flight back home. He took the elevator up to the 12th floor where his suite was located.

"Bri, we gotta go, baby," he told her. When he didn't get a response, he yelled her name a second time. Again, no answer.

Walking into the spacious room, he saw two men with guns and they pointed them directly at him. Bri lay hogged-tied on the floor with a swollen face, and cuts from being slapped a few times with a pistol.

"Hi, K-Do, long time no speak," Luc said, walking towards the frightened man.

"Luc?" K-Do's voice got raspy. Keith and Luc always had a good bond. K-Do was also Luc's best man when he married his sister.

"Don't look so surprised. You knew comin' out here would be a risk," Luc said, as Lil BD posted up, waiting for Keith to make a false move, so he could blow his brains out of his skull.

K-Do did know coming to Miami was a risk but he tried to stay lowkey except he'd gone out to a few clubs with Bri.

"That shit ain't got nothing to do with me, Luc."

"Who told you that, K-Do? It's too late for you to play the surrender game," Luc added, looking at Bri on the floor, trying to get out of the double hog-tie.

"I can make this right, Luc, just let me and my baby mother live, and if nothing else, let me live," K-Do begged.

"She is marvelous when you find her?" Lil BD asked. He noticed K-Do shaking and he looked as if he would break down in tears.

"Due to the circumstances, there is no way out of this unfortunate event. That's why you never grow too familiar with anyone. Familiarity and vulgarity goes hand in hand," Luc said, before aiming his gun at Bri.

Boc! Boc! Boc!

Keith fell to his knees when he saw the bullets enter Bri's head.

"Lil BD, you know what to do with him." Luc pointed at K-Do who, by now, lay on the floor crying. Then, five big muscle-bound Haitians entered the room to finish the job.

PORT OF SPAIN, TRINIDAD

Kamla had been waiting five days for her cousin K-Do to come back from Miami. She called his and Bri's phone but never got an answer.

The doorbell rang and Kamla went to answer. Wearing a Dolce & Gabbana robe and slippers, her thick thighs and manicured feet made her look like eye candy.

Kamla opened up the first box and jumped back when she saw Bri's dead body inside, wrapped up with Kamla's favorite kind of pink roses spread over her.

"What the fuck is this?" she asked one of her security guards who spoke the Caribbean Hindustani language.

"Get that bitch's body out of my fuckin' house!" Kamla started to worry about K-Do. The next box had holes in it as if a wild animal rested inside. She told her guards to open it.

K-Do was inside the box tied up, but he was still alive thanks to the holes that allowed him oxygen to breathe. Luc had spared his life but he'd told Lil BD to place a small note in the box with him.

Kamla had her brother untied and got him water and food because he looked weak and dehydrated.

Minutes later, he was able to talk as he cried in front of Kamla, the most unemotional person he'd ever meant.

"He killed Bri and spared me, Kamla."

"It's okay, you're home now," she said, just as she spotted the small note on the floor. She picked it up and read it out loud to herself...

"Next time, there will be no mercy. There is only one reason why he's alive. I'm very certain I will see you soon, and don't think about sending any cargo to my port unless you're giving to charity." The note was signed: *Luc, your one and only.*

Kamla placed the letter in her robe pocket. She was highly pissed as she stared down at the wedding ring Luc had given her.

"They killed Bri," K-Do cried, snapping her out of her daydream.

"Shut the fuck up with all dat! At least you're alive! Now get your punk ass up and cancel that Miami cargo. Luc is on to us. He must've had someone on the inside," she said. Little did she know, Luc and the owner of the Port of Miami had been doing business for years, and anytime someone from certain country's wanted to ship shit in, Luc would be the first to know. That was how he'd found out K-Do was in town, and having the heads-up gave him time to plan the move.

"I don't get it. We just locked in the deal and lost my baby mother all because of you." K-Do was getting frustrated because he was overwhelmed.

"She was dead weight anyway. The only thing she was good for was breastfeeding, and maybe, sucking dick. Cancel that order!" Kamla said unbothered. She walked off laughing at the fact that Bri was dead and K-Do was alive.

Kalma knew her brother K-Do was a pussy but she still treated him with tough love.

DOWNTOWN, MIAMI

MALONEY WATCHED TV in his hotel room—the four rooms beside his were occupied by his soldiers. A few weeks prior, he'd thought he had the drop on Lil BD, but he hadn't expected to see Vina there. She'd put a monkey ranch in his plans and he'd come so close to killing them both.

At the present moment, reflecting on a new plan was where his head was at mentally.

Seeing Vina had fucked up everything because he knew how she got down, and she didn't play games. The only thing on his mind was figuring out how the hell the Costa Rica Cartel and the Haitian Mafia had linked up. Maloney's only way of surviving was to find help because he didn't have enough manpower to face both families.

Romell Tukes

CHAPTER 26
CABRINI GREENS PROJECTS, CHI'RAQ

Spike climbed out of his new Jeep SrT8 that he'd drive whenever he thought he'd be involved in a high-speed chase with the police. It was a beautiful day outside so the whole city was out and about looking for shit to get into.

When niggas saw Spike coming, they all tightened up as if they were all doing something, especially his little cousin Pop who ran the projects with his crazy crew.

"What's up, folks?" Pop asked, while embracing his older cousin, whom he hadn't seen since his last re-up.

"How's it looking out here?" Spike asked, seeing a few fiends rushing in and out of the dirty buildings.

"Everything good—money moving and we out here smoking on nigga's dead homies," Pop said, referring to his OPPs. He pulled out a blunt of weed.

"You got the money ready for tonight?" Spike had only gone out to make sure Pop had everything in order for the product when it arrived from Miami by way of Boss.

"You don't gotta ask me that, bro."

"I do, because you're known for fuckin' up." Spike reminded him about the hundred thousand he had come up short on during the last re-up. Two of Pop's shooters had got locked up and needed bail money so Pop had dipped in the re-up loot.

"That was a different story. I had to get the gang out."

"Next time use *your* money for dat but how's your mom?" Spike asked.

"Working and talking shit about you." He laughed.

"Damn, folks, she still think I'm the reason you out here in dese streets, huh?" Spike knew his aunty thought he was the reason Pop was hustling in the streets and moving keys instead of in college playing basketball.

"Yup."

"You know the truth," Spike joked.

"Oh, I forgot to tell you … Last night, me and the gang went out to the strip club VIP and I overheard niggas talking about Juball coming home."

"Fuck that nigga! He know what's up wit' us 'cause we been smokin' on his dead homies." Spike had already heard Juball was coming home and he was more than ready. Spike and Juball beef went back from their early teens when the two men used to have shootouts on the expressway.

"A'ight." Pop looked over his shoulders and realized the hood was starting to get flooded by fiends looking to get high.

"I'ma let you do what you do and I'ma slide to the crib in South East I'ma call you when it's time."

"Bet that, bro," Pop said, before making his way in the projects to make sure everything was moving good.

Spike pulled off still thinking about how the city was about to turn up when Juball got home, especially after he'd recently killed Juball's brother, Heavy.

***

Vina and Lil BD had spent the whole day together. They'd done everything from tennis to horseback riding and they had just got done eating at a nice restaurant.

The two hadn't seen each other in almost two weeks and it felts like forever. Vina had just returned from Miami earlier that morning and Lil BD had been at her private runaway waiting for her to land.

He had begged her to leave the goons she'd come with, at a hotel, something she'd never done until she did it for him.

Vina had worn a sexy Fendi mesh bodysuit that barely covered her nipples, ass crack, or pussy. As a result, Lil BD had kept a hard-on all night looking at her body parts.

After dinner, the two left the restaurant and Vina invited Lil BD back to her penthouse suite at the hotel. Doing so was definitely something she would never think of doing with anyone else, but she loved the connection she'd made with Lil BD and she didn't want the night to end.

"I can't believe you beat me in tennis earlier. You move fast on them little legs," Lil BD joked. Vina walked over to the in-house bar and grabbed two champagne flutes.

"You still owe me $100,000 for beating you loser," she joked, and at the same time, kicked off her heels before joining him on the couch.

"I thought you was joking." Lil BD grabbed a glass as she popped the bottle of Armand de Brignac Brut Gold and poured them both a glass.

"I don't joke too much."

"When you left I missed you a little and I came to realize something very important."

"What's that?"

"I want and need you." His words caused her to choke on her drink.

"Are you sure?"

"Yes," he said, "I wanna love again and you're the only woman I desire because our bond is rare. You need me as much as I need you, Vina, and I'm willing to do whatever I have to do to show you I'm the one for you." Lil BD saw the overwhelmed look that etched itself across her face.

"I want you too," she replied. Then she leaned in for a passionate kiss. Their tongues did the French tango as their mouths remained connected. "Make love to me," she moaned as her fingers parted their lips.

Both stood up and it seemed as if they were in a race to see who could undress the fastest. After they got naked, Vina sank to her knees and stuffed his hardened penis into her hungry mouth. She wasn't a pro at sucking dick but she didn't mind being taught a thing or two.

"Uhhmmmm," Lil BD moaned as she licked and sucked on his cock, giving him a great, sloppy blow job. When he felt his cum building up, he knew it was too early in the game to nut; besides, he wanted to give her a night to remember.

"Hold on." He stopped her.

"You don't like it?" she asked.

"I loved it but I wanna fuck the shit outta you." He made her smile.

She knelt in front of the couch and rested her arms on the seat cushions before looking over her shoulder at him. He positioned himself behind her.

"Ohhhh shit." She squirmed as he placed the tip in her tiny, slippery hole.

Lil BD couldn't believe how tight and good she felt and he had to hold himself back. "Damn, you feel good," he said, as she groaned and gasped, as he thrust dug deeper inside her. It wasn't long before her pussy began to spasm uncontrollably, and before she knew it, she'd released an orgasm.

Switching positions, Lil BD sat her on the couch and she spread her legs open wide. He kissed her sweet, hard nipples and nibbled on each one, twirling his tongue round and round on it.

Vina's kitty cat purred as it became drenched with her natural cream, leaking all over the couch. Next, he attacked her clit with his long tongue, cultivating the erotica tension she felt building right before she exploded again, all over his face. Her pussy walls convulsed around his fingers as pure pleasure surged through her body, and never did she ever imagine she could feel so damn good. She pushed him away unable to handle his head game because she was about to go crazy.

"You're the devil," she told him, as she grabbed his hand and pulled him toward the bathroom so they could go fuck in the shower before having a night cap in bed.

The sex session was on another level with them, and that night, they fell in love with each other sexually.

CHAPTER 27
TAMPA, FL

Chloe treated herself to a day out, alone at a coffee shop, then she had set up a treatment at a new Japanese spa/resort in Tampa, FL.

She couldn't remember the last time she'd been able to sit down, drink coffee, and just read a book. She'd worn a hat, sunglasses, and a Chanel sweat suit to blend in.

"Nice try but I could point you out in a crowd of models." The voice made her look up and when she did, she saw Louis.

"If it's ain't the ghost of Casper with the broken dreams. Heard you was in New York until they ran you outta there, now you back in Miami. You're really crazy," Chloe stated, remembering the time when he'd come to her for allies and to give up his family for the price of nothing. She knew he was a snake and the worst type—poisonous.

"I like to move around just like you. Maybe I'm here on business?" Louis suggested, and then took it upon himself to sit down.

"Well, what the fuck do you want?"

"I think it's time we come together and take these muthafucka's down once and for all. We're stronger together than apart."

"What makes you think that?"

"You have the manpower and the connection," he said.

"And what is it you have?"

"I know Janella, Luc, and Boss inside out. We can mastermind plots, kill'em all, rob them, and take over their drug trade," Louis said, realizing he'd piqued Chloe's curiosity.

"Sounds good, Louis. I tell you what … we can team up, but you've got one time to cross me or even look like you wanna betray a bitch, and I promise you, I'll take my time cutting your dick off." Her voice was stern and harsh.

"See you real soon partner." He stood up and fixed his dress shirt.

"Please don't say that—it really doesn't sound right."

"My bad," Louis laughed out. Then, he disappeared just as fast as he'd appeared.

Chloe hoped agreeing to deal with Louis again had been the right choice. She knew he could get to the Haitian Mafia better than anybody since he'd been one of them until they rejected him and crushed his ego. Chloe would keep a close eye on him just because she knew his rep.

MIAMI BEACH, FL

DANILO WALKED BACK UPSTAIRS leaving his smoking room where he'd smoke cigars and get his thoughts together. One thing that had been on his mind lately was Luc, and the fact that he was still alive.

Sending Pablo out to kill Luc seemed like a task the young man wasn't equipped to handle, but Danilo knew the Haitian Mafia wasn't easy to kill or target.

Every day, he thought about his beautiful daughter, Lela's death, and he missed her and his grandbabies daily. When Lela and Luc got married, that very morning he'd told Luc if anything ever happened to Lela he would come for Luc. When his baby girl died he swore to himself he'd fulfill his promise.

"Daddy," Kristina said, as they stood around the kitchen with the maids and cooks.

"Hey, baby, I thought you were at school," he stated.

"I'm done with my class and it's so boring in the dorm. I came to spend the rest of the evening with you," she said, hugging him.

"A whole day? I don't know if I can keep up with you," Danilo replied, knowing a day with her would make him feel like a teenager again.

"I promise you, today will be fun. We're going fishing."

"*Fishing?* What made you come up with that?" he asked. He and Lela used to take Kristina fishing with them when she was a little girl.

"Just for old times' sake," she replied.

"Okay, well, let me a call Pablo and get ready," Danilo stated.

"No point in doing that," she said, tasting the stew one of the cooks had made.

"Está todo bien." Danilo asked *'if everything was okay'* in Spanish. He wore a worried look.

"So he's been dealing with this pretty girl from my school. I think they go out or something because they've been spending time together every day. I like her. Es Una nina muy bonita," Kristina said, telling her father Amor was a very pretty girl.

Danilo understood why Luc was still alive and why his product in the east coast had been showing up late for the past week. Being in the game so long, Danilo knew women, marriage, and relationships could easily and slowly push a person off their duty by making them lose focus.

PALM BEACH COUNTY, FL

RUSH AND HIS CREW were up in the club having fun in the VIP surrounded by women, bottles with sparkles, and they had drugs for everybody. Having to bury his brother was hard but Rush didn't consider niggas friends or family if they were snitching or stealing from him.

Rush had his men toss his brother's decapitated head on Big Hulu's turf to let him know how he was coming. Seeing his mother cry at his brother's funeral was the hardest thing he'd ever had to do in his life.

He had been in the club for a while when a dude seated in the VIP room across from him caught his attention. The dude was alone and dripping in diamonds, and he appeared to be watching the crowd. Because he'd done jail time and was deep in the streets, Rush was always aware of his surroundings.

"I'll be back, cuz," he told his Crips as they entertained the loud women who were all looking for a come up.

Coolly, Rush walked over to the man's section. He didn't see any bottles, any women, or killers, so he could only assume the man had to be a cop, OPP, or an out-of-town nigga.

"No disrespect, cuz, but I couldn't help but notice that you are in a club with no bottles or women," Rush said. The man looked at him with his cold eyes. Rush knew off the rip he had to be a killer because his eyes reflected his dark soul.

"Very observant, Rush. I like that," the man spoke loudly over the blaring music.

"How you know my name?"

"Have a seat, please."

"Fuck all dat! Who the hell are you?" Rush replied.

"I'm the man who's gonna make you richer than you *think* you are. The people you work for are gonna cross you just like they did everybody else who crossed their path. Never be blinded by a big booty and a smile, Rush."

"You still ain't tell me who you are."

"I'm from the Haitian Mafia and my name is Boss."

"Oh shit," Rush mumbled. He'd heard of the dangerous crew plenty of times.

"Take my card and call me, so we can sit down and talk, Rush. I need you on the team. I see your loyalty," Boss said, before turning to leave, "enjoy your night."

CHAPTER 28

SOUTH BEACH, MIAMI

Since Boss had gone back home to Chi'Raq for a few days, Luc had had gone out to Miami to link up with Lil BD.

Climbing out the lime green Lamborghini Urus SUV, he saw his shooters pull up behind him in a Sprinter.

A few months prior, he'd opened a new, fancy Caribbean restaurant right on the South Beach strip. He waited to get a bite of his favorite Caribbean meal before meeting Lil BD in Overtown, a place located across the bridge.

"Nikko!" Luc shouted for the manager he'd hired a while back. He'd helped Nikko out by giving him a job and getting him off the Haiti Streets so he could live a better life in the states. Luc knew firsthand how hard it was to live in Haiti—people were dying from starvation and shit was real back home for his people stuck in poverty.

Seeing the restaurant empty seemed odd because last time he'd visited there had been close to sixty people out and enjoying the Caribbean food. The back door opened and Nikko came out with a gun to his head with Louis following behind him. Luc went for his pistol and aimed it at Louis.

"What cha gonna do now?" Louis said, as he made his way closer to Luc, walking passed the ovens and counters. A big grin covered his face.

"You crossed the family, Louis, and we've done anything except cater to your selfish needs and wants," Luc said. Nikko's eyes swelled with tears and Luc could see his fear.

"Fuck the family! You and Janella tried to take over the family and leave me the handyman job."

"*Handyman job*? Nigga, you had a big position in the Mafia."

"No, I had what y'all wanted me to have," Louis replied.

"You think trying to team up with the OPPs is gonna help you win the battle?"

"Fuck the battle! I'm trying win the war!"

"First you gotta win the war within self!"

"You think Janella can be trusted?" Louis laughed.

"More than you."

"I see why. Her sidekick a fake, bitch ass nigga," Louis said pushing Nikko foward.

"Suck my dick, punk ass nigga. I should've been killed yo' snake ass," Luc said.

"Well, you got the chance now," Louis said, before blowing Nikko's head off then firing at Luc.

Boc! Boc! Boc! Boc!

Luc ducked the bullets and sent two shots back. They grazed Louis and almost took off his head.

"Ahhh," Louis groaned in pain, before Luc's men busted in the restaurant and shot the place up. The shots fired almost hit both Luc and Louis.

Seeing all the gunmen enter, Louis crawled out of the back kitchen the same way he'd entered an hour earlier. He made it out through the back and hopped on his motorcycle. He raced off as Luc's men ran outside behind him. There were people all over the place and some of them had heard the gunfire while others had not due to the music playing at the event showcase on the beach.

SOUTHSIDE, CHI'RAQ

BOSS POSTED UP on a new, white Bentley Continental GT V8, right on O-Block, located at the corner of 64th and MLK Drive, also known as Parkway Gardens.

Niggas were deep and everyone seemed to envy Boss' busted down watch and his diamond choker chain that was worth $500,000. Boss loved being back home, but he knew deep down, if he didn't relocate and leave the city, he'd soon be dead, or in prison.

Boss had a condo in the downtown area. Nobody knew about it, so whenever he got home-sick, he would go back to the city. One thing about Chi'Raq Boss loved, was that it was unlike any other city he'd come across.

Spike stepped out of a building with ten youngins and all of them stared and admired the Bentley. The niggas ain't know who

Boss was but they knew he had to be somebody big if he was talking to Spike, the Prince of the City.

Everybody in Chi'Raq had heard of the Chi'Raq Gangsta's because they were city legends just like Hoover, Jeff Fort, Hobo, and Willie Vice, to name a few.

"You ready?" Spike asked, approaching the car he was digging.

"Yeah, I gotta go visit Malik's grave site," Boss said. His late friend was killed one night in Miami when they were supposed to meet, and today was his birthday.

"Gratitude, bro. I heard a lot about him," Spike said.

"Yeah, unlike Animal, he kept it solid until the end. But I wonder whatever happened to his girl, Kylie. She came down to Miami to put in work wit' us and when he died, she disappeared," Boss wondered aloud, even though he knew Spike didn't know.

"Never heard of her."

"How's business?"

"Good, besides the little beef shit going on. But you know how that goes out here, " Spike said, noticing the Bentley getting a lot of attention as it cruised through the hood.

"There is a saying I'd like to share, and it's know how to use your enemies. A wise person finds enemies more useful than the fool does friends. You may one day owe your greatness to an enemy," Boss told him.

"Some shit it's no turning back from, folks, you knew that your crew flipped the city and all y'all OPPs and enemies are dead."

"*Most* are," Boss corrected him as he drove into the graveyard to pay respect to Malik. He remembered when he had Malik's body shipped back to Chi'Raq to get buried. That shit had hurt him to the core.

Romell Tukes

CHAPTER 29

TUNJA, COLOMBIA

Lexus and a few of her most elite men came out to Colombia to meet with Alar of the Tunja Cartel Family. They reached out to her a few days earlier and asked her to come out to Tunja to discuss an important issue. Lexus supplied the majority of the Colombia Cartel Family, from Florence to Barranquito, even Peru and Bolivia. She was the biggest supplier in Central America besides a family in Brazil and Argentina.

Growing up, she used to love coming out the Colombia with her father who had a few properties that he'd left to her. Now that Santos was dead, just taking a step in Colombia felt awkward, and she would be left with a gang of emotions she didn't want to deal with.

The SUVs drove down a narrow path that went up a small hill to Ajvaro's Mansion. It was surrounded by several armed security guards who awaited her.

Mark had wanted to come but she needed him to purchase a new crib in the Summerland Key since she disliked staying at one location too long due to safety measures.

"Everybody can stay out here. I'll be quick," she said. She exited the truck and proceeded to get patted down for weapons, by Alvaro's goons. She knew Alvaro didn't allow his guests to bring weapons into his home, and Lexus respected that.

Stepping inside the high-ceiling, eighteenth-century French declaration of the home gave off a classic theme.

"Lexus," Alvaro's wife said, seeing her in the living room with her husband. Alvaro's wife, Anna, was a beautiful Colombia woman whose brother ran the Palmyra Cartel family.

"Hey, Anna, I see you got some new lips," Lexus said, when she noticed that Anna's lips were much, much larger than they'd been the last time she'd seen her.

"Yeah, I'm glad you like. I'll be leaving now because I have to go get the children." Anna kissed her husband. But he looked pissed.

"What's the problem, Alvaro? I left the states to come all the way out here." Lexus took a seat. She watched Alvaro pour himself a drink and check his watch for the time.

"When you took over the family business you took responsibility to control the State of Colombia. Your father was a magnificent man and an appealing businessman." Alvaro looked at her as he talked.

"Where is this going?"

"The other night, my people went to go pick up the shipment you sent me but when they arrived, my men were put in an inconspicuous position," Alvaro said, as eight armed men walked into the living room.

"What the fuck is going on?" Lexus became angry when realized Alvaro's men had surrounded the room. She knew how dangerous and ruthless Alvaro was.

"My man got killed and the product was stolen. You and I were the only two who knew when that shipment was arriving, so it looks like a set-up to me, and all fingers point at you," Alvaro stated.

"Why would I rob you of my own fuckin' shit? Especially since I never received the money from your end." Lexus had a point and her reasoning made perfect sense. It had never dawned on Alvaro that the product hadn't been paid for yet.

Normally, Alvaro would get the product then send the money to Lexus and it was business as usual for both sides.

"If you didn't do it, who did?" he asked.

"Did anybody see the gunmen or how they even got to the airstrip?" Lexus asked.

"The driver said he saw a bunch of men with dreads," Alvaro stated.

"*Dreads*?" With a dumbfounded expression, Lexus looked at him as reality set in.

"Yes," he confirmed, "and I believe one of them left a Haitian flag at the scene," Alvaro informed her. Now, he couldn't help but wonder why the Haitians would want to rob him.

"I'll find out who's behind it and I'll send you another order as soon as I get back to the states," she said.

"It's not about the drugs, Lexus, someone came on my turf and disrespected me and my family."

"Alvaro, I told you I would take care of it."

"Lexus, if I find out you had something to do with—

"Stop right there, Alvaro, because I don't give a fuck who you are!" she snapped, "I take threats very seriously, so like I said, *'I'll handle it and will send you a new load in a few days'*." She stood up to leave without saying another word.

Alvaro slammed his glass into the wall. He was upset because he felt like Lexus, someone he'd trusted, had been down with the entire robbery.

Lexus left the mansion cursing herself out because she knew, most likely, Boss was the culprit behind Alvaro being robbed. He knew all of Lexus' clients because at one point and time, he would assist her in going over her black book where she had written down all of her supply routes. Boss must have written her clients and routes down elsewhere, or maybe he'd even memorized them. Whether or not she would admit it, Boss had hit her in the head and he'd stabbed her right in the back.

PALM BEACH COUNTY, FL

IT WAS EARLY IN THE MORNING when Boss and Rush met up at a local beach. Boss had sent Lil BD to Colombia with some of his goons, to rob Alvaro's shipment, and the robbery had been a success. He knew Lexus would be heated but she had to get a taste of her own medicine.

Rush had reached out to him and informed Boss that he needed to speak with him about the brief conversation they'd had at the club.

"I love the beaches," Boss said, as the waves washed up and down the beach's shore.

"Facts, bro, but thanks for coming out. I thought about everything you said but I need to have a clear understanding of who you are."

"Fair. Me and my brother are from Chi'Raq. The two of us started from the bottom out there. When we found out about our

Haitian ties, our lives changed for the better. We hopped in the Miami drug game while still holding down Chicago. We ran into a whole lotta beef out here with other families from the Colombians, Cubans, and Mexicans. We need people like you on our team because you're loyal. However, you seem to be loyal to the wrong people. Chloe is the snake of all cobras, and Hitler turned on my little brother—they were best friends," Boss said.

"How do I know your crew will be loyal to me and mines?"

"You don't, but actions speak louder than words."

"A'ight, I'm down, bro," Rush agreed.

"Good. I'll introduce you to the family real soon but everyone already knows about you," Boss told him.

"*Me?*"

"Yeah, your father was down with Luc back in the day before he caught his life sentence," Boss stated.

"My dad got sent away when I was a kid." Rush wondered what type of relationship his dad and Luc had, whoever *Luc* was.

"I don't know but Luc is really the one who scoped you out first. You were in prison."

"He might be the nigga who was putting money on my books every month," Rush said, as he remembered the name Luc popping up on his account—ten bands would be deposited every month during his bid.

"Maybe … I don't know about that but you'll be getting up with him tomorrow."

"Hitler will be coming to pick up his money next week. I think I got a plan for cuz." Rush looked up and saw a group of sexy women walking by them in bikinis that showed off their phat asses.

"Holla at Lil BD 'cause he's looking forward to meeting you anyway."

"I got one question," Rush said, as the wind rocked his long dreads.

"What's up?"

"Why me?" Rush had wanted to know the answer ever since meeting Boss in the club. It had to be something besides loyalty. He had done his own research on the Haitian Mafia so he knew they were big time people with a small circle. At the end of the day, they could've chosen anybody they wanted.

"I was gonna let Luc Explain it to you but we're family. Your dad was mine and Luc's first cousin," Boss said.

"Damn, that's crazy, cuz. I never met anybody on my dad's side of the family."

"Well, you have now, cuz. Welcome to the Haitian Mafia." Boss gave Rush a hug before leaving. He knew Rush needed time to let everything soak in.

Romell Tukes

CHAPTER 30

HIGHLAND BEACH, FL

Jess had a beach house in Florida that he only visited twice a year. When Chloe told him to come out to Miami, he took her to the beach house which sat on the waterfront.

Chloe climbed out of his bed, ass naked, and checked her phone. She had nine missed calls from Hitler. Her and Jess had been up all night having sex because they couldn't get enough of each other. She had even let him fuck her in the ass for the first time. Her goal was to get him hooked so when she needed him, he'd come running.

"That was a crazy night. I've been waiting to see you since the boat party," Jess said, as he lit up a cigar.

Reaching for her clothes that lay on the floor, Chloe bent over and exposed her shaved pussy.

"You know how to hit the right spot with that curve, daddy," she replied.

"What do you got planned for today? I want to fly you out to Mexico," Jess asked, hoping she would be willing to enjoy the trip.

"I'm sorry, I can't not today. I have so much to do."

"Okay."

Gun shots could be heard downstairs and Chloe and Jess snatched the two MP4 weapons that had been laying on the side of the bed.

Tat! Tat! Tat! Tat!

Downstairs, the gunmen surrounded the home going at it with Chloe and Jess' crew. Chloe fired a few bullets at the shooters and recognized one of the faces. It was Mark.

Tat! Tat! Tat! Tat!

Jess got hit in his shoulder by Mark and fell down the stairs. Chloe saw the gunmen airing out the goons and Jess' guards. She dashed across the hall and into the bathroom and found an escape route. It was every man for himself so she jumped out of the window and onto the sandy beach.

The shooters were waiting for her outside but they were so focused on the front area they didn't see Chloe running down the beach like a mad woman. As she ran, she could still hear the loud shootout going on in Jess' home but there was no way she was about to turn around and go back.

MIAMI UNIVERSITY, FL

AMORA COULDN'T WAIT UNTIL her English class was over so she could go meet Pablo. Two days ago Amorashe'd asked him to be her boyfriend and he'd gladly accepted.

Most days she spend with him at his apartment or the dorm. They hadn't had sex yet because she wanted to take her time. She also didn't want him to think she was a hoe or anything like that.

When the professor ended the class Amora almost flew out of the room trying to be the first one out. She had been naturally smart her whole life and made straight A's in all of her classes, nothing less, and that was without studying.

Pablo texted Amora's phone and told her to come to his crib because he had a surprise for her later that night.

Normally, Amora and Kristina would go out for lunch or to the school gym, if it wasn't packed with muscle-head girls and boys from school. Kristina was so cool, they would spend the night in each other's dorm room.

Amora hopped in her Benz that she'd parked right in front of the English building. Driving off, she played the newest hit song Beck G. Looking in the rearview mirror, she noticed an SUV trailing closely on the Benz' rear bumper.

"What the fuck? Like, get off my ass!" she yelled out loud. The Miami license plate read *D.D.C.*

Paying the truck no mind, she figured getting on the highway would be a faster way to Pablo's crib. She hopped on the highway and drove toward a small bridge. When the Benz made it on the bridge, a big SUV rammed into her and almost forced the car over the guardrail.

"Ahhhhh!" she screamed, as she watched the Spanish man in a suit ram into her Benz again.

After the second ram, her car flipped over the bridge and onto the lower level. Three cars slammed into her upside-down car before the Benz caught on fire. Civilians stopped to help and some parked to watch and record the crazy car wreck. The ambulance and police rushed to the scene and rushed Amora to the hospital not knowing if she would live or die.

JACKSON MEMORIAL HOSPITAL, MIAMI

Pablo received a call from his little cousin Kristian who claimed a student at her school had seen Amora get into a bad car accident that caused her car to blow up. Once he found out what hospital she was at, he rushed to her aid.

He ran into the hospital and gave the first nurse he saw Amora's name, and she told him Amora was in the ICU.

In a panic, Pablo took the stairs to the next level and looked for her room, all the while praying his girlfriend would be okay. He had never given a fuck about life, but Amora was changing that about him.

He found room 205 and saw several nurses surrounding Amora as if they were trying to save her life. A nurse in a surgical outfit came out of the room.

"Excuse me, Miss … is she okay?" He wanted to go inside the room so badly but he knew they had a job to do.

"Luckily, she's okay and she's going to make it, but someone really tried to take her out. This wasn't an ordinary car accident at all and I've seen my fair deal of car crashes," the pretty lady told him, taking off her gloves.

"So, she's definitely going to make it?" he asked again.

"Yes, she's got a few broken bones and dislocations but she'll be fine in time," the nurse said, before walking off with a strut in her step, hoping the handsome man was watching.

Pablo paced up and down the halls trying to make sense of everything. Unfortunately, he'd have to wait until Amora healed to speak with her about it.

CHICAGO HEIGHTS, CHICAGO

Spike bought his mom and little sister some jewelry to show them how much he cared for them because they had been down with him since day one. The month before he'd bought his mom a new house and himself a new Porsche SUV. Spike didn't let a soul know where his family lived which was rule number one of the streets.

Parking next to his mom's Cadillac, he went inside to surprise them. The front door was wide open which wasn't something his mom did so he knew his sister had to be leaving. When he walked into the living room, he found his mom and sister dead on the floor, in a pool of blood. Spike had tears in his eyes looking at the blood-bath. He could hear the sirens coming as looked at the gunshot wounds to their heads.

CHAPTER 31

PALM BEACH COUNTY, MIAMI

Rush was on his way to meet Hitler to drop off the re-up money he had in the trunk but today would be a different type of drop. Next week, he would have to go out to Haiti for the Haitian Mafia meeting and he couldn't wait. Rush couldn't believe he had family in such big places.

A couple of nights ago he met his cousin Lil BD who had brought him his first load and it was the first keys he'd ever laid eyes on. With his crew backing him up, Palm Beach was all his—the only roadblock in the way was Big Hulu.

Hitler wanted to meet Rush in a biker bar parking lot, and for some strange reason, he would always request the oddest places to meet up. The bar parking lot had a few bikes and cars parked out front so he waited near the back entrance. Seconds later, he saw two Cadillacs swerve into the lot and guessed it was Hitler when he flashed his lights.

Rush got out to greet Hitler and found it weird that Hitler was traveling with goons since he'd always press the issue with Rush and requested he always come alone when dealing business.

"Rush, my bro, what's good?" Hitler's energy was different and he appeared happy and joyful.

"You ready to get this over with?" Rush asked, not feeling Hitler's vibe.

"Before I collect my shit, I just thought I should let you know, me and my wife won't be needing your assistance from here on out."

"What? I don't understand." Rush looked confused.

"Let me make it clear for you." Hitler turned back, waved at his goons, and they exited the Cadillacs.

"Oh, it's like that, cuz?"

"Facts. You was only the helping hand, bro. Now I can take over Palm Beach and lock shit down—well, right after I kill you. Of course, we can't forget that." Hitler pulled out his gun.

"Now I know why they call you Hitler."

"Big facts." Hitler smiled.

"That was a nice little set up, but I think you forgot one big thing," Rush stated, looking at all the guns aimed at him. He showed no signs of fear.

"Who, me? Because it looks like this shit worked out perfect."

"Expect the fact that I got Haitian ties," Rush said. Hitler's face turned upside-down when he heard the word *Haitian.*

Niggas popped up from all over the parking lot with all types of guns from ARs to MPS's.

Tat! Tat! Tat! Tat! Bloc! Bloc! Bloc! Bloc!

Rush and Lil BD was on Hitler's ass firing left and right, but missing as he ducked, zig-zigged, and spun. He did every trick in the book as bullets came at him from all over.

Lil BD's men wiped out Hitler's shooters within seconds, leaving a parking lot full of bodies, including a few of their own.

Early that morning, Rush and Lil BD had come up with the plan to ambush Hitler, but Lil BD forgot how fast Hitler was on his feet.

SAN JOSE, COSTA RICA

Vina's palace was always heavy secured with guards and there was a large brick wall surrounding her home. She had been home since last Tuesday, taking care of her business dealings with her Chilian clients and a Uruguay crime family who complained about everything.

She had just woken up and threw on her exercise gear so she could hit the gym in the lower section of her guest house, next door from the main house. Keeping her body in shape had been Vina's main focus during her free time. Working on her legs and abs was a must.

The maids were already in the kitchen preparing her post-work out meal and her hot cup of steamy coffee was awaiting her on the counter.

"Muchas gracias." Vina thanked her maids who only spoke Spanish.

Coffee and green tea was her daily drink because it was the best fat burner. Walking to the guest house she answered a FaceTime call from Lil BD on the first ring because he hadn't heard from him in two days.

"Hey, papi. I miss you," she said, smiling into the screen as the sun beamed on her perfect skin.

"Cuant ma costna?" Lil BD asked 'how much', showing off his learning skills since he had been learning the Spanish language for her.

"A lot, but when you coming out here?" she finally asked, At first, she wasn't comfortable with letting him know where she lived.

"You trust me now?"

"Maybe, come and find out."

"That sounded nasty. Let me find out you ready for another long night," he joked.

"Shit, I'm ready for a lifetime with that masterpiece." She walked into the gym which was the same size as Planet Fitness gym.

"I'ma fly out tomorrow."

"I'll be here. I'ma go exercise and call you back."

"A'ght, later," Lil BD hung up. She had a big smile on her face, and she was feeling freaky. She couldn't wait until he pulled up.

Romell Tukes

CHAPTER 32

St. Vincent, Caribbean

Maloney had recently reached out to the Trinidad Mafia for a sit down. It would be his first time making a bold request like that, and he was nervous. At the end of the day, business was business and Maloney knew about the serious beef with the Haitians and Trinidadians, so she figured it would be a perfect time to join forces.

Kamla agreed to meet Maloney on common turf. St. Vincent's boat dock on the tourist side, in public was the perfect spot just in case Maloney had any funny ideas. If that be the case, she would blow his head off right in view of the public eye.

Maloney moved when Trinidadians robbed Louis then ended up robbing him. To this day, he was still in his feelings about the loss.

Kamla and a large boat of gunmen cruise up to the dock to spy on Maloney and his Egyptian men who were all highly trained in martial arts and weaponry.

"Maloney, what do you do?" Kamal extended her hand as Maloney shook it. Seeing Rowley step off the boat, he recalled hearing a lot about the vicious man who could kill a man with just his bare hands.

"Thanks for coming out. I know it was a big surprise to hear from me out of all people," Maloney stated.

"True indeed, especially after we robbed you once we got word you had dealings with our enemy." Kamla smiled.

"So you know that was my product?"

"Of course, but let's put the past were it should be."

"Fair." Maloney felt his anger rise but smiled despite it.

"How can I help you? The call seemed a little urgent," Kamla stated.

"From my understanding, you're having trouble with the Haitians and us Caribbean people need to stick together," Maloney talked professionally.

"You're white," Rawley said.

"I'm more Caribbean than you. I just have White skin and blue eyes." Maloney's tone got real menace as Rowley hit a trigger spot.

Living in the "Bahamas his whole life, he had always been looked at differently because of his skin complexion, and it bothered him a lot.

Kamla tried her best not to laugh at her brother's comment but it was too funny. She had to let out a chuckle then a cough to play it off.

"We will forever have beef with the Haitians and it won't stop." Kamla hoped she hadn't wasted her day to talk about the Haitians.

"I want to help," Maloney added

"Why?" Even Rowley wanted to hear this one.

"I've been in Miami trying to find them and I just don't have enough manpower to go against them or the Costa Rica Cartel." Maloney realized he'd got their attention.

The Costa Rica Cartel? Vina? Kamla asked, She took off her sunglasses and hoped she'd misunderstood his comment. Vina was the most powerful, youngest woman in Central America, and that could lead to bigger problems.

"Yes, I saw her with the young kid Lil BD. There's something big going on and I think together we can take them out and conquer them," Maloney suggested.

"Deal. We need a snake like you in the field, Maloney. Contact Rowley for anything you need and we will aid and assist you in any way we can," Kamla agreed.

"I'll be in touch," Maloney said, turning to leave with the guards.

"He can't be trusted," Rowley told his sister, as he helped her onto the boat.

"Who can you really trust nowadays?" She gave him a look before telling to captain to pull off.

"You have a point."

"I know." She looked out into the ocean. Rowley's phone rang.

Kamla heard Rowley yelling over the cell phone, and at the same time, tears began to formed in his eyes.

"You good?"Kamla asked.

"They killed Missy," Rowley said sadly.

"Oh nooo!" Kamla couldn't believe it.

"Her body was chopped up and placed in a tea pot that had a Haitian rag inside." Rowley tried to remain strong but it was hard.

Kamla's mind flashed to Luc. It was his motto to chop people's family members up with something he'd stolen from them. Stay strong," she told him, as the ocean wind blew her long hair.

"I'll kill all of them!" Rowley's tone changed as a demon crawled inside of him.

Summerland Key, FL

LEXUS' NEW MANSION HAD BEEN CUSTOM designed from the ground up. The place had an office, library, kids play forum, art gallery, floor-to-ceiling stone, slab walls, glass windows, three floors, eight bedrooms, six master bathrooms, a walk-in shower, a spacious loft with skylights, green lawns, and a built-in poll inside and out doors.

Looking into the backyard, she watched the nanny she'd hired interact with the cute, little one-year-old baby boy. Lexus loved her son with all she could imagine. Having a child was a big step, and even without help, she'd managed to be a mom and dad to the little baby. He was joyful and happy.

When she wasn't out handling business, she took care of her little man, giving him all the attention he yearned for. Entering motherhood had made Lexus see a lot of things differently.

Growing up the way she had, she never had to worry about material things, but losing her dad had taught her to stay prepared at all times and for anything.

She went out to join her baby boy outside to play and decided to give the nanny the day off.

Romell Tukes

CHAPTER 33

PALM BEACH COUNTY, FL

Big Hulu entered his baby's mother's, Omaha's, apartment after a night clubbing with his boys. He could have easily left the club with the dancers but when Omaha texted him she was wearing his favorite lingerie, he had to see what she had in store for him tonight.

"Damn, baby." Big Hulu didn't know she could look so good. Her thick thighs and flat stomach were toned perfectly.

Omaha had recently got her body weight down and she was looking and acting differently. "I knew you would rush home." Stepping on her tippy toes because she stood a mere four feet, she kissed his lips.

"I wouldn't dare miss the chance to be up in that pussy." He slapped her on the ass before sitting down on the couch.

Omaha got on top of his fat ass.

"Hold on, my daughter sleep?"

"Yes, big daddy."

"Oh okay. Do that thing I like when you deep throat it while humming on it."

"My pleasure," she said, going down on him, but Big Hulu's fairy tale was short-lived when he felt two guns aimed at back of his head.

"Relax, big boy, this is gonna be fast," Rush said, creeping out from the kitchen,

Big Hulu saw Omaho jump up and smile before she jumped in Rush's arms.

"Fuckin' snake-ass bitch!" Big Hulu was furious—his own baby's mother had set him up.

"Sorry, fat boy, but me and Rush go way back, since pre-K. When he came to me, I was more than willing to help him set it up to fuck his whole gang one by one. Classy shit," she said, gazing at the crazy look on Big Hulu's face.

"You had a good run, bruh. I respect it, but these bitches be a real nigga's down fall," Rush said. Omaho shook her head up and down.

"We can get money together," Big Hulu said, trying to devise a quick game plan to stay alive.

"It's a little too late for that, playboy, I lost a lot of good soldiers thanks to you," Rush said.

"Fuck you then! "Big Hulu shouted.

Boc! Boc! Boc! Boc! Boc!

"That's the end of him,'" Rush said, lowering his weapon.

"Now we can finally be a couple." Omaha jumped up and down as if she'd won the lotto. Rush looked at her as though she was really crazy.

"*Together*?" Rush asked.

"Yes, like you promised me when I agreed to help you set this up," she told him. She noticed the confused look on his face and it changed her mood.

"Walk with me in the kitchen real quick, baby girl. Look, I have to keep it real wit' you."

"You wanna move out of the states, I know. Let's do it, I'm down wit' you till my casket drop," she said, ready to leave her daughter and life for him.

"Omaha, slow down. This ain't gonna work 'cause I could never trust you, dummy. I literally just watched you set your baby's father up," Rush told her as she began to cry.

I did it for you," she pleaded for his love.

"Sorry."

"What you sorry for?" she cried out, just before Rush lifted his gun and fired two shots in her pretty face.

"We need to go," Rush said, seeing a little girl come out with a teddy bear in her arms.

"Go back to bed," Rush told her. Because he looked just like her dad, the little girl did as she'd been told. Rush saw a familiar trace of himself in the little girl but he brushed the thought from his head. He had been fucking Omaha for years, but surely if she'd been pregnant by him she would've told him, or wouldn't she?

He had to fly out to Haiti for a meeting the following day and he was nervous. He had to take care of Big Hulu so Palm Beach County would belong to the Haitian Mafia.

PORT-AU-PRINCE, HAITI

Janella sat at the head of the round table looking young, black, and beautiful. Her dreadlocks were neat, shiny, and long. Rush couldn't believe this was his family as he looked around the table to see Boss, Lil BD, Janella, and Luc.

"Let's welcome our new family member, Rush. We have been watching you for a long time, and you're exactly what you presented yourself to be—honorable, loyal, smart, and deadly. Your father was my dad's favorite, besides myself, of course" Janella said, making everybody laugh.

"Who lied to you?" Luc added, as the maids brought more food and drinks to the table.

"All jokes to the side, you got your dad's blood in you which is Haiti blood. We're strong and unbreakable," Janella added.

"Thanks for everything. I plan to expand the family and make power moves," Rush said .

"Elevation is what we are on," Lil BD added.

"Now that we have Vina with us, Chloe, Kamla, and Maloney should be easy bait," Luc added.

"You just killed Rowley's wife, the voodoo bitch?" Janella asked, eating a salad.

"Yeah."

"How is that helpful?" Lil BD asked.

"You worried about the wrong thing. To really destroy a man, you have to start from within inside," Luc said, not feeling Lil BD's vibe. One day they were cool and the next they were on the rocks, and Luc didn't like it.

"Now that Palm Beach is locked in, we should focus on Tampa and Broward County," Boss said, trying to speak on the business aspect of things, since Luc and Lil BD would go back and forth on bullshit all day.

"I haven't heard from Danilo in a while. I want you to check in on him," Janella said, as everybody nodded, talking about whatever came to mind. They enjoyed the whole weekend.

Romell Tukes

CHAPTER 34
SOUTH MIAMI, FL

Luc drove the Rolls Royce in silence. Normally he would be listening to jazz music or Caribbean jams, but he was lost in his thoughts. This morning, Luc took a trip to his late father's house. Nobody knew about it besides him, and he'd found a letter.

When Luc read the letter, he couldn't believe what was revealed, and he knew the information could really be a game changer to the Haitian Mafia. When he read the letter, he felt as if his father had betrayed him.

He was reconsidering and re-evaluating if he should tell everybody, but he knew what it could stir things up and they were finally starting to come together.

His car needed an oil change and he'd seen an auto car shop on the corner and figured it would be a good time to have it changed. An hour from now he had to meet Janella because she would only be in town for short period of time.

He placed the letter in the glove compartment and thought about how his dad had truly been a lunatic with a good heart. Still, he'd done things nobody understood. Luc praised his father for being so magnanimous as a businessman of exceptional wealth, influence, and power. His dad had done more for Haiti than any president or government could ever imagine.

***

Mark was out taking care of something for Lexus, and she was really starting to get on his nerves with her bossy and arrogant demeanor.

The news of Big Hulu's murder had fucked up his drug line in Palm Beach, and now Lexus had him on a mission to go see Hialeah and Wynwood for a new location. The Haitians had no ties on that side of the city.

Mark saw a new two-tone Rolls Royce parked in an auto shop getting an oil change, but the person standing next to it was what really got his full attention.

"Ain't this a bitch, papi, got you now," Mark said to himself, pulling out a gun from under his seat.

Pulling the Benz into the parking lot, he smoothly crept out of the car, but Luc had somehow seen him out of the side of his eyes and quickly reacted.

Bloc! Bloc! Bloc!

Mark swiftly ducked and moved out left, towards a minivan and used it as a shield.

Boc! Boc! Boc!

Luc dipped on the side of the building as two of the workers at the shop got hit with Mark's bullets.

"Bring it!" Luc yelled with a bedlamite look in his eyes. He fired and hit the van.

Mark snuck behind a dumpster and got a clear shot on Luc.

Boc! Boc! Boc! Boc!

Luc saw the cop flip off the bike and knew it was time to get the fuck out of dodge. He hopped in his Royce Rolls and raced down the block, going in the opposite direction of the police.

Mark was still there, firing his gun at the police cars arriving and he'd already killed two more as he tried to get away on a motorcycle he'd stolen from the shop.. The police shot Mark twice in his upper back and nearly knocked him off the bike, but he managed to keep his balance and haul ass into the Homestead area giving way to a high-speed police chase.

He was able to get away on the bike due to the fact that he had been one of the best biker boys in Colombia.

NORTH MIAMI, FL

JANELLA LEFT HER GOONS in the hotel lobby and some were left outside. She walked into the bar/restaurant to meet with her guest and longtime client. The bartender gave her a curious look as she made her way to the table in the back.

"Long time no speak," Janella told her guest of honor.

"I almost had her," 'the man with a cast on his left arm stated.

"*Almost* never counts. I thought you out of all people would have to the ability and expertise to kill a low-level bitch like Chole, but I guess she gave you a taste of her venomous pussy. I heard it could fuck up any man's head," Janella told Jess who sat across from his connect.

Janella had known Jess for a while. Her dad used to do business with his dad. So, the Haitian's had always had a good rapport with the Mexican Cartel's top families, and Jess' family was high in rank.

"I set up a shootout at my beach house so she would think it was a hit. I even killed some of my men and got shot in the process, but before I could finish her off, she ran on me. I was so mad, I killed five of my men that night," Jess explained. He took a quick glance at Janella's sexy breasts which he could see through the flimsy button-up she'd worn.

"This is why you never send a bitch-nigga to do a real nigga's job, especially a tender-dick one," she said, as she dug into her purse.

"I promise to make it up to you," he begged.

"It's straight, Jess. I'll handle it," she told him, "you had your chance." Janella pulled out a log blade and sliced his neck wide open and began stabbing him in the head as she went into overkill mode.

When she finally thought Jess was dead, she took the napkin off the table and cleaned her bloody knife off as she looked at Jess's slumped body, repulsed by his carelessness. She fixed herself up and walked up to the bartender and gave him a stack of money that she'd pulled out of her Birkin bag.

"Sorry for the mess," she said in a nonchalant manner, before turning and strutting off, as if nothing had happened.

JACKSON MEMORIAL HOSPITAL, MIAMI

Amora couldn't wait for the day to arrive because she was finally going to be released from the hospital. Since the car accident, her life had been on pause while she laid in a hospital bed watching dumb ass reality shows. Pablo had visited her every day and because Kristian considered them good friends, she had even gone to check on her a few times.

Gathering her clothes and laptop, Pablo entered the room to help drive her back to the College. Amora was still a little bruised up from the crash but it wasn't too bad, and she'd seen worst scenes.

"You ready, beautiful?" Pablo asked, making her smile.

Amora loved the fact that even when she was at her ugliest, he managed to make her feel as if she were the prettiest girl in the world, and that meant a lot to her.

"Yes, give me one second," she said, "I gotta find my class schedule."

"It's in the car," Pablo told her.

"Oh, I guess we're ready to leave then. I already signed the release papers. By the way, I have to buy a new car today, so can you take me to a car dealership?" she said, before she started rambling a blueprint of things she needed to do.

"Chill out," Pablo said, "you can use my Audi. Right now, you just need to focus on getting better." He grabbed some of her things and proceeded to carry her bags outside to his car.

Inside the car, Amora took a deep breath and laid her head back. "Thank you for being here," she said sincerely.

"Sure thing, and as you would say, 'why don't we go get a bite," Pablo joked as he pulled off.

"When those guys tried to ram me off the bridge, I just knew I was going to die. They looked like Mexican Mafia with suits on. I was scared shitless," she admitted.

That was Amora's first item telling him what had taken place and he hadn't even asked because he wanted to wait until she was ready.

"*Mexicans*?"

"Yes, I was shocked too, but I saw murder in their eyes when I looked in my rearview mirror. I saw the DDC license plate and that was it. When the police questioned me, I could've said something, but where I'm from, that's a big no-no!" Amora spoke freely but Pablo's mind was shuffled elsewhere.

"Did you say *DDC License plate*?" he asked.

"Yes."

Pablo knew there was only one crew with a DDC license plates and the offenders were his own family members. DDC stood for Danilo's Dominican Cartel.

"Stay at your college for a while and I'm gonna look into it."

"I don't want you to hurt nobody," she said, having seen enough violence in New York.

"I'm doing whatever I have to do so I'm able to protect you," Pablo told her, while driving to Miami University. He wanted to get straight to the bottom of it because something wasn't right.

Romell Tukes

CHAPTER 35

DOWNTOWN, CHICAGO

Spike had gotten picked up the previous night while at his stepsister's house. He had gone out after he saw his face on the news that announced he was wanted for questioning about the murders of two known Maniac Latin Disciples from Humbolth Park. Burying his mother and sister had taken his soul from him and he wasn't the same Spike no more.

The police had him at the Grand Central Homicide Headquarters downtown, and they were trying to connect him to the murders. A Black cop entered the room with a smirk on his face, holding a cup of hot Starbuck's coffee.

"Spike, what's up? It's good to see you again. I told you I would nail your ass one more time, and this is the big payoff I've been waiting for. If you had paid your dues, maybe you wouldn't be here with that dumb ass look on your face," Hartford said.

Everybody in the city who had a big name paid Officer Hartford to keep the police off their asses, but once their money started drying, he would send their asses straight to jail with all types of crazy charges.

"I can understand why you don't want to talk, but you got a few seconds to give up your drug connection and then I'll let you walk out of here and charge you with a couple of keys and guns," Office Hartford said, and waited for a reply.

"Boss," Spike said.

"What was that?" Office Hartford could barely hear him.

"You remember the Chi'Raq Gangsta's?" Spike asked.

"Nigga, who the fuck don't! They flipped this city upside down but I heard they were all dead or some shit."

"Nah, they moved to Miami and they're doing it big, man. I swear they're moving big weight. I've been copping with the boss for a while now," Spike said.

"I'ma look into it and get back at you, because I got some people who want him and his little brother, Lil BD."

"Can I go now?"

"Not yet, give me some more people," Office Hartford added.

"Juball killed my mom and sister three weeks ago in Chicago Heights."

"I heard about that."

"He did it," Spike scolded.

"So that's why you killed two of his homies at Humboldt Park?" Officer Hartford saw the look on Spike's face.

"I ain't do shit. It was two of my soldiers and I'll tell you where they at. I just need to get the fuck out of here, please," Spike begged.

"Let's get you out of here, Spike, you gave me more than enough." Officer Hartford uncuffed Spike and led him out of the police station through the back door.

"Thanks, OG," Spike said, about to walk off.

"I'ma drop you off 'cause I don't want nobody to see you leaving here," Office Hartford opened the undercover cop car door for him.

"A'ight." Spike climbed in the backseat as Office Hartford scoped the area.

"I gotta make one stop on the west side real quick," Officer Hartford said, before turning up the music he cruised to.

Minutes later, the uncover car pulled up in Spanish Cobra hood and Spike wondered what the fuck was going on because the SC were his OPPs.

"Give me one second." Office Hartford got out and acted like he was about to walk off but snatched open the back door and grabbed Spike out before putting a gun to his head.

The block was dark and only two hoodlums were out— they made a loud bird call into the building.

"You set me up!" Spike yelled, as the dirty cop walked him into the building where Juball and his people were waiting.

Six Spanish men came out to let Officer Hartford inside, seeing their rival at gunpoint.

"Juball inside," one of the soldiers said, knowing his boss would be happy.

"Juball where you at?" Officer Hartford yelled, as he entered the apartment.

"Today is my lucky day. I saw y'all out the window." Juball and two gunmen came from the back of the trap.

"I got him, now where is my $100,000? Nobody knows a thing and the city is still looking for him. I sneaked him in and out of the station undetected," Office Hartford said, ready to collect the bounty on Spike'd head.

"Perfect." Juball ice grilled Spike.

"He ratted on you, Boss, the Chi'Raq Gangsters and he's vicious," the dirty cop said.

"Damn folks, you get down dirty, but Officer Harford we have a problem," Juball said.

"Oh no we don't. I did my part," the cop stated.

"We do. I don't trust you and I can't do business with a person I don't trust." Spike lifted his gun and fired two bullets in Officer Hartfield's head, dropping him.

He'd found the perfect opportunity to run, but when he took three steps, bullets rattled his back and took him down, killing him instantly.

"Y'all clean this shit up and meet me on the Southside. It's time to reconnect the city," Juball told them before leaving.

Juball was a MLD Maniac Latin Disciple from the Westside. He was the gang leader with a million-dollar mind frame. He'd recently come home and wanted to take over, but Spike was in his way. Plus, Spike had killed his brother, so his first day home, Juball had killed Spike's family. He'd had the Latin King and Latin Jivers on his team after he killed the leader of the Spanish Cobras the night before. And when he'd gone to jail, he'd taken over the SC turf and formed a bigger crew. The only thing he needed now was a plug.

Romell Tukes

CHAPTER 36

MIAMI BEACH, MIAMI

Pablo entered Danilo's mansion where he saw a few guards standing around chatting, paying him no mind, giving off weird vibes.

"Where's Danilo?"

"Office," one of the guards stated, giving Pablo the evil eye.

Pablo had gone by to find out what was up with Danilo's people and why they had tried to run Amora off the road. However, it could've been a big mistake, but one thing young Pablo knew about his uncle was he didn't make mistakes.

The office door upstairs was in the cut and one would truly miss the French, wooden doors that blended in with the French wooded walls on the second floor.

"Uncle Danilo?"

"Pablo, enter," Danilo shouted, recognizing his nephew's voice.

"What are you up to?" Pablo played it cool, trying to catch on to Danilo's energy.

"I'm blessed. Where you been at?" Danilo asked, looking up at him. He laid the Wall Street newspaper down.

"I been outta sight for a little."

"Everything okay?" Danilo had a worried look planted on his face and Pablo couldn't help but realize how fake his uncle really was.

"I just been doing a lot of thinking about my life and future," Pablo admitted.

"You're losing focus. Maybe you should go back to the DR for a while and clear your mind so you can get back to what you're good at," Danilo said, picking the paper back up.

"This shit is getting old, and it's draining me at a young age. I can't even sleep at night no more because of all the murders." Pablo admitted something he never talked about to anyone.

"You will be fine. That's part of the game but try living with those nightmares for fifty years." Danilo gave off a light chuckle.

"I'm not you and I make my own decisions in life, just like you made the choice to try to kill my girl."

"You were losing track of business. This is a cartel family run by structure, and that girl had your head so far stuck up her ass I had to get rid of her. Plus, you need to be with your own kind anyway. I did you a favor, "Danilo said.

"My own kind? This ain't the fuckin' 50s or 60s. I don't judge people by their skin. This is a new era in life and I'm done working for your racist, wrinkled up ass!" Pablo got up to leave.

"You leave this house and you're not a part of this family any longer, and I will have your head, I promise," Danilo said, coughing as he became upset.

"Handle your business and I'ma handle mine. You know how I'm comin'. Oh yeah, the girl is not dead." Pablo walked out and slammed the door behind him.

Outside, Pablo saw a SUV with a big dent in the grill. It pulled up with DDC license plates and he stopped as two men got out.

"Big O and Carlos, how y'all get that dent in the grill?" Pablo asked them.

"Oh, your uncle sent us on a mission to drive some bitch off the road and kill her, but we knocked her car off the bridge and killed her. You should've seen that shit," Big O said. Both men looked Mexican but they were Dominican, full-blooded.

Without another word, Pablo pulled out a pistol.

Boc! Boc! Boc!

Pablo shot both guards in the forehead then got in his car and drove off before a few gunmen rushed outside and fired at his car.

For the past few days, Pablo had been thinking about living a better life since working for his uncle was a headache. He'd been feeling like a slave ever since he was a kid, and that's how long he'd been working for Danilo. Pablo never had a real life outside of killing and drug dealing which was draining him now. He knew giving up the game would be hard, but he had a few million dollars in the cut and some properties.

***

152

Chloe and Louis had just got done giving each other oral sex for nearly four hours. Louis had never ate a bitch's pussy that tasted so yummy.

"That was fun." Chloe brushed her teeth in the low-grade hotel Louis was staying at.

"I know why niggas get hooked now," he stated.

"You lucky I ain't let you fuck me, papi. I saved your life," she joked.

"You may have saved your own life," he shot back.

"Why are you staying here?"

"I know they'll never find me here," he said, "Luc would expect me to be at a fancy hotel or condo somewhere in North Miami," Louis told her.

"I see now, papi, but what's your plan?"

"To be real, I'm just going day by day, trying to catch them slipping out there."

"You have to be smarter than that when dealing with our family, especially Janella... that bitch is sneaky." Chloe sat in his lap.

"You don't even know."

"I have to go, but I'll call you soon, Mr. Nasty." she smiled.

"I'll be here." Louis pulled out his laptop out, and for his next mission, he decided to do some homework.

***

Mark just arrived in the capital of Colombia to visit some family and take care of some business for Lexus while she was in Miami. He had dreaded this trip for many reasons, and one, of course, was Lexus doing the most and complaining,

On the flight there, Mark had come up with the idea to just kill Lexus and take over the family business. That was one reason for coming out Colombia.

Walking to a nearby cab, he paid no attention to the three vans parked outside waiting on someone. Right on point, the van doors slid open and a bunch of masked men jumped out with assault rifles and snatched Mark off his feet.

A crowd of civilians stood by and watched Mark get beat up and kidnapped, but this was an everyday thing. So, when the vans peeled off, people went back to their daily lives.

TUNJA, COLOMBIA

"MARK, LONG TIME MY FRIEND. HOW long has it been? A year or two?" Alvaro took the blindfold off Mark's eyes. He'd been tied to a chair, in a large barn built like a warehouse.

Mark looked around at the manpower. There was wild animals in cages, including three bulls.

"Alvaro."

"Yes, it seems to me there has been an issue. And since Lexus, your master, refused to help me figure out who robbed me, I knew you would." Alvaro took a red towel and placed it on Mark's face.

"I don't know, but it wasn't me!" Mark yelled.

"Of course, but who are the Haitians and what type of business do they have with you all?" Alvaro pushed Mark's chair into the bullpen and the bulls circled around waiting on rec time—which was Mark.

"Boss is Lexus' husband, but they're at war with us, Alvaro. I swear we ain't rob you, the Haitian Mafia did. Lexus could have helped but I didn't," Mark cried.

"Thanks Mark, but you and Lexus are a team so I have to kill you. But, no worries, I'll give you a nice, fast death." Alvaro locked the cages and watched his bulls kill Mark in less than five minutes.

CHAPTER 37

BRENTWOOD, MIAMI

Boss spent an hour at the local park, jogging late night while listening to a King Von album, and his favorite song on the playlist was "Crazy story".

He lived two blocks away from the park so he walked home just to check his surroundings. Boss leased a nice home in Brentwood, low-key in the cut. Nobody would ever imagine that a person of his status would be living there.

The day before, Spike's cousin had told him someone had killed Spike, and that he had some money that belonged to Boss. The news was a little shocking, but Boss knew in Chi'Raq, one day you could be in the field drilling and the next you could be the person getting drilled. When he headed back to Chicago, he reminded himself to look into Spike's death because the kid was loyal and about his paper. What seemed odd to Boss was how Spike's cousin didn't have a sound of grief in his voice.

Walking inside his crib, he smelled a familiar scent— Chanel perfume. Boss took out his Glock .22 and cocked it as he crept toward the kitchen.

"I came alone, Boss," Lexus said, sitting at the kitchen table, dining on Henny he'd had in his cabinets.

Boss still had his gun out wondering if he should just kill her now and get it over with. "I should've blowed your fuckin' head off, stupid bitch!" he spat, before lowering his gun.

"But you didn't."

"I still can any second. Make wrong move and you'll see," Boss told her, as he stared at the white, satin dress made by Gucci. The dress gave Lexus an appealing glow.

"When I heard you and your family had killed my dad, I was hurt at first. I didn't want to believe it because I ain't know how. My love for you was out of this world. The pain I was bearing at the time led me to kill Malik then you were supposed to be next, but something in me wouldn't allow me to kill you." She took a sip as she cried.

Boss had always known it was Lexus who had killed his best friend, but he couldn't prove it. The night Malik was supposed to meet him, he showed up to a crime scene, and something in his gut told him it was payback for Hector Santos' murder.

"You got sixty seconds to exit, if not, I won't hesitate to kill you in the memory of Malik." Boss had a seriousness written all over his face,

"Two more things before you count down ... you stole my drugs I sent to Alvaro." She looked at him.

"What about it? Get it back in blood," he said.

"The only issue is I'm not the one trying to get it back. You have Alvaro and his people on your ass now and he wants time, Boss. They killed Mark and I'm sure he told them your name and told them about us. Alvaro knew your people robbed him, but I had told him before he killed Mark that I would handle it, but he's taking matters into his own hands," she stated, getting out of the chair, taking her last sip.

"Let him come then. We gonna take him then you, and I should have poisoned that drink. What classy lady drinks Henny like water?" He made her crack a smile.

"Never said I was classy when you married me," she said.

"Don't remind me! Now get the fuck out," he told her, as Lexus got so close to his face, she could feel his breath.

"Before I leave, the reason you're not dead is because I want you to meet your son first." She touched his long dreads and she remembered that he used to have braids when they first met.

Boss was speechless as she walked off and closed the door. He tried to add up the time period of the last time they'd had sex and he knew it could be possible. He ran outside to stop her but Lexus was gone with the wind.

DOWNTOWN, MIAMI

HITLER CAME OUT TO HAVE A DRINK and meet new niggas he could use to open up shop in Miami. Chloe told him to stay away from the hood. The Haitians were large in numbers because most likely they worked for the Haitian Mafia.

Tonight, he'd spoke with two females who hustled, and made plans to link up with Hitler to do business. Losing Rush was a big, low blow because he was clocking in some serious paper in Palm Beach.

Seeing Lil BD come to Rush's aid was the surprise of the year and he couldn't help but feel bad for what he did. Growing up, him and Lil BD were like day and night. The two had did everything together in Chi'Raq—rob, killed, fucked the same bitches and rocked the same clothes. He knew Chloe had played a big part in crossing his friend but Hitler grew jealous of Lil BD when he came to Miami.

When the war between Lil BD and Boss broke out, Hitler was right there by his side. Hitler knew Chloe was cheating on him with other men because she'd been acting different and less sexual. Sometimes, at night, he would try to break into her phone but she would be on point like an alarm clock and wake up.

Taking his last shot, it was time to leave Wet Willy's and go home since he'd completed his mission for the night.

The BMW SUV he climbed in had the push-to-start button but before he could press it, Hitler saw him.

"I knew one day I would catch up with you, bro," Lil BD said, from the backseat, putting a Colt .45 handgun at Hitler's head.

"I guess you just got to me before I got to you," Hitler shot back.

"Money can't buy loyalty, Hitler, 'cause when the money leaves then what?"

"Nigga, fuck the money! It was about friendship," Hitler confronted Lil BD.

"*Friendship*, huh? Look where friendship got a nigga. I often used to tell myself, loving a nigga in the streets is like diggin' your own grave," Lil BD stated.

"I won't beg for my life so kill me."

"That was the plan away."

Bloc! Bloc! Bloc! Bloc!—Hitler's head landed on the steering wheel and Lil BD jumped out of the BMW and got into the Honda that pulled up with two Haitian chicks inside.

The two women Lil BD was with were the women Hitler approached trying to get on his team. They worked for the Haitian Mafia in transporting drugs. So, when Hitler told them he was a kingpin looking for workers, they called Lil BD.

Hitler had been in the bar for a few hours when Lil BD saw who the women were talking about and pointed out Hitler's SUV to him. Now, with his ex-friend out of the way, Chole was next up on the bucket list.

BROWARD COUNTY, MIAMI

PABLO HAD GONE OUT OF THE HOOD to tell his men he was out of the game and they would need to find a new plug. He had two areas in Broward on lock, but now someone else could have it. He also needed to go out to the DR soon—his workers could cut ties with him after he collected his money.

Parking in front of a complex building, three dudes were standing around, and one of them was his boy, Juga. Juga sold for him. It started to rain a little so Pablo grabbed a hat out of the back seat.

"Juga." Pablo hopped out of the car as everybody looked his way.

When Juga saw Pablo, he had to do a double-take because the rain started to come down a little harder. Pablo peeped something awkward but when all of them reached toward their lower backsides, he beat them to the punch.

Boc! Boom! Boc! Boc! Boom! Boom!

Pablo shoot two of them and one took off when his gun jammed. Seeing Juga as he crawled toward the doorway prompted Pablo to run over to him.

"Who made you do this?" Pablo stepped on Juga's fingers.

"Ahhhhh, some nigga name Danilo. He said you a rat and put $300,000 on your head, Pablo, I'm—

Boc! Boc! Boc! Boc!

Pablo got back in his car and drove off highly upset that Danilo had thrown dirt on his name by calling him a rat. Working for his uncle for so long, he knew how he moved and the way Danilo thought, so he was about to use that to his advantage and make his next move really hurt Danilo.

Pablo was going to get Amora. He wanted her to put school on pause for her own safety. They had taken their relationship to another level and he really loved her. He felt as if he'd known forever instead of a short period of time.

Driving through the rain he could see there would be a Hurricane hitting the city that night and he needed to hurry up and find Amora so she could get the fuck away from Miami University.

Romell Tukes

CHAPTER 38

WESTSIDE, CHI'RAQ

"Juball!" Yellow shouted from Juball's baby's mother's crib. Three shooters, including Yellow, were surrounded by seventeen Haitian killers. The Haitians had popped out four-cars deep, and Yellow got starstruck as they demanded to see Juball.

"Why are you calling me? I told you Juball saw what was going on and froze."

Boss climbed out of the Bentley he was in across the street.

"You Juball?" he asked.

"Yeah, why the fuck are you and them dread heads disrespecting my block?" Juball played tough, but for the first time in a long time, he really was scared.

"Take a ride with me to La Bambra. I know your fat ass like to eat," Boss said, as Juball walked across the street.

"I'm Puerto Rican. I love La Bambra but that still don't tell me who you are," Juball stated, waiting next to the Bentley.

"Get inside," Boss said one last time and got in his car. This time, Juball followed and got inside the comfortable car, and the Haitians disappeared off his block.

Juball had been holding shit down on the West and Northside of the city. Since Spike was out of the picture, he and other crews were fucking up the city by trying to rob and do anything to eat because it was a drought of coke and dope.

"You must not be from around here," Juball said.

"I'm Boss and you owe me a few mill."

"I owe you? Nah, you got the wrong nigga. Hold on you said *Boss?*"Juball asked finally catching his name.

"You killed Spike?"

"I never heard of that goofy papi, sorry." Juball chuckled.

"Look, I was supplying Spike before you killed him."

"So you the nigga he ratted on to the cops? If I ain't kill Spike or Officer Hartford, your ass would be in a jail cell. Next time you should be cautious who you supplying," Juball said, as Boss pulled over.

"I see you talk a lot, but I know what you did and that's the only reason why you still alive, bro. I did my research on you and I like how you handle your shit in these streets, so I wanna give you a position and a chance of a lifetime," Boss said.

"You that GD nigga from Chi'Raq Gangstas?" Juball had heard a lot about Boss—some said he was a billionaire, some said he was dead, and others had forgotten about the city's legend.

"Yeah."

"Damn, folks, this is big."

"I want you to form an ally with every gang in the city and supply them Blacks and Spanish's. You one of the most respected dudes out here and if you can control the drug trade, you can come up overnight. There ain't no plugs in the city, and I don't fuck around out here no more. I'm down there in Miami, but I want you to supply all the gangs. Get two dirty cops on your team and some more loyal gunners to protect you, 'cause you gonna be seein' some real paper soon," Boss explained to him.

"I'm down."

"Okay, welcome to the new era of Chi'Raq Gangstas," Boss told him.

"Oh shit, so I'm 'bout to start a new chapter of Chi'Raq Gagnstas?" Juball was excited.

"Nah, I'm startin' it," Boss corrected him, "you like the cap," he clarified.

"That'll do too, shittt." Juball's grin was so big, it's a wonder his lips didn't split. He knew for a fact, things were about to change in Chi'Raq.

BOGOTA, COLOMBIA

LEXUS AND TWO MEN RODE in the backseat of a limousine, headed to Alvaro's wife and children's place of stay. When she'd found out Alvaro had killed Mark, he'd started a war, and she wasn't one to war with— not ever. Telling Boss about their child had taken a lot out of her, but she knew it was the right thing to do. At the time, she thought Boss would kill her for telling him Malik had been murdered at her hands—the look in his eyes had said it all. Unbeknown to her, Boss had known all along she'd done it, but hearing it from the horse's mouth was all he'd ever wanted, and now his mind could, somewhat, rest.

"Did the Neiva Family place the bomb in the truck as I requested?" Lexus asked her men.

"Yes," one man answered, another shook his head in the affirmative.

"Perfect." She popped open a bottle of Henny and drank from the bottle, something she'd learned from her husband. The guards looked at her as if she were a manic, but they knew she was crazy.

The limousine stopped at a ranch style house where a few luxury cars and children's toys could be seen out front. Lexus got out and told the limo driver to pop the trunk. She rushed to get the grenade launcher, which was so heavy, she almost fell over.

Two little children could be seen walking into the barn while playing in the backyard. She was glad because she had a child of her own and didn't feel comfortable killing children. So, she took the opportunity and aimed it at the house, but as far away from the children as possible.

BOOM! The house blew up and fire and smoke was everywhere. The impact of the blast caused Lexus' body to fly to the ground and it fucked up her right eardrum. The hood of the limo was nearly blown off and the windows shattered. The driver of the limo was clearly shaken up. Before getting back in the vehicle, Lexus could hear the children screaming and crying which was evidence of their fear. At least, it was confirmation that they'd survived the blast.

She left like a thief in the night and no one would be the wiser that she was ever there. With that taken care of, she felt much better.

TUNJA, COLOMBIA

ALVARO HAD JUST GOTTEN THE CALL that informed him that his wife and brother both had been killed in a big home explosion. As fast as his feet would take him, he loaded up the goons and drove to Bogota.

The guards in Bogota assured him his daughters were both safe and alive, and for that, he was thankful. The night felt like the worst night of his life. Losing his wife was crushing his heart every second he thought about her. What didn't seem right was the fact that his brother had also gotten killed at the house. Lately, he had been seeing a brother he'd grown distant to getting closer with his wife.

Unknown to Alvaro, his brother and wife had been having an affair for over two years. Alvaro had always been busy and barely had time for her, which had left her horny and lonely.

There were a few people in mind he thought might've been responsible for the explosion—the Naiva crime Family or perhaps Lexus in an effort to avenge Mark's death. Whoever had done it would pay with their lives. And at that very minute, he swore to himself there would be so much bloodshed, he would be able to fill the Pacific Ocean.

CHAPTER 39

CARIBBEAN SEA

Kamla was enjoying the beautiful day on her boat, tanning and getting some private time away from bullshit and family business. Feeling the sun beaming on her skin felt so good she didn't want to go back home.

The Haitian Mafia was really getting on her last nerve and since Rowley's wife had been killed, calming him down so he could think rationally, was like talking to a deaf baby. She understood his rage and she'd promised him payback soon. For now, they just needed time to form a successful plan.

"Kamla, we have trouble," the boat Captain yelled.

"What the fuck you mean?" Kamla raised up in her sexy Louis Vuitton bikini. Before she could realize it was a boat attack, shots rang out.

Tat! Tat-Tat! Tat-Tat-Tat!

The captain of the boat flipped the thief over and into the water with two head shots. Kamla had left her weapon upstairs but for some reason, she paused and look out into the water. What she saw was several boats filled with gunmen holding Haitian flags.

When she saw Luc pull up to her boat in a jet ski, her heart stopped and her blood rushed to her brain. He climbed onto her boat and yelled her name over and over again.

"There you go, Queen!" Luc found Kamla standing up with her arms crossed over her chest indicating she was pissed off.

"I'm going to fuckin' kill you, Luc," she said, with malice in her tone.

"I already know, but listen, I think it's time we talk."

"What? Are you fuckin' kiddin' me! You just killed the boat captain then you murdered my brother's wife! That wasn't smart, not to mention, K-Do's wife!" Kamal looked at him as if he'd suddenly grew two heads.

"Should I go down memory lane with you because you're no saint!"

"Luc, what do you want?"

"I need advice," he said, seeing her eyes raise in curiousity.

"Advise? Not you."

"Really."

"What is it?" She got serious.

"My father left me a letter and he mentioned that Francisque speaks very highly of you." Luc saw her smile.

"He always liked me."

"My pops had another life and my family didn't know about it. He basically had two families," Luc told her.

"What? That's crazy!" Kamla couldn't see Francisque as the type of man to keep secrets so important away from them.

"He also told me a few secrets that would destroy everything I've been working so hard to build."

"Sometimes you have to destroy to rebuild, Luc."

"I know, but this type of shit can cause bloodshed and there are some snakes in the grass," Luc told her.

"I could have told you that," Kamla said, as she heard more jet skis arriving from a distance. Luc heard them too and figured Kamla had backup coming

"Your people are late," Luc told her.

"Those are not my people. I thought they were yours." The two looked at one another and knew someone was trying to kill two birds with one stone.

"Come with me." Luc grabbed her hand and ran down the stairs as the OPPs grew closer.

Tat-Tat! Tat-Tat Tat!

Luc's crew fired shots at the incoming enemy who had Tobago flags all over the boats and jet skis. They arrived forty deep ready to kill the two families they hated the most.

Kamla grabbed the AR-15 assault rifle before jumping on the back of Luc's jet ski with him. They fired at the Tobago men while driving through the mayhem. It looked like the cold war on the ocean. Luc's men were getting hit up and the few who could get away, followed him as his jet ski raced on the water. trying to get back to a safe location on the land.

PANAMA CITY, PANAMA

Today was Vina's birthday and Lil BD had taken her on a surprise trip to Panama City. He took his girl to an island resort for an experience she would never forget.

The hotel section was for the soulful sojourner and adventure-seeking culinary enthusiast. It was a luxurious lifestyle with the island's natural setting. The restaurant was serving an array of locally inspired small plates of wonderful food. The quintessential beach escape was what both of them needed.

"Baby, you made my week. How did you even know Panama was my favorite place?" she asked, laying on the private beach with white sand, enjoying the sight of the crystal clear water.

"I didn't, I just always wanted to come out here." He joked.

"Whatever."

"How about I give you this massage now?" Lil BD pulled out a towel.

"Sounds good to me." She turned to lay on her belly.

Lil BD poured oil on her back. He took off her bra and looked around to make sure they were alone. He started from the top and worked his way down to the bottom of her back. Looking at her ass poking up, gave him a hard-on.

"Uhmmmmm…" She felt good as he rubbed his manly hands all over her.

"You like it?"

"Yes, but I wanna fuck."

"Right here?"

"Yes." She rolled over and took off her bikini.

Lil BD didn't hesitate to do the same when he quickly undressed. He slid into her tightness and started to make love to her right on the towel. Her screams could be heard all over the island. They made love for an hour and when a few tourists caught them in action, they didn't bother to stop; instead, they continued to go hard.

PORT-AU-PRINCE, HAITI

JANELLA HAD A LARGE GARDEN in the backyard of her mansion and she loved planting flowers. It was her most relaxing time of the day and she actually considered it her meditation hour. Afterwards, she planned to hit her private gym for forty-five minutes of an intense cardio session with two of her fit guards. One of the guards was handsome and she'd been considering giving him some pussy but he'd just started working for her.

Janella couldn't even remember the last time she'd sex but it was about time she let someone break her walls down.

Luc told her he was going to see if he could get Kamla because he had an idea she was on the boat. She told him it would be a bad idea because she knew what type of mastermind bitch Kamla was and she didn't want her to brainwash her brother again.

Lately, Luc had been acting very odd and strange but that was her brother. Kamla couldn't believe how hard it was to get a hold of Louis. It was starting to drive her crazy a little but one thing about Louis was that he would always pop back up at the most awkward moments.

Checking her watch, it was time to exercise. She loved to keep herself as busy as possible to keep her mind at ease.

CHAPTER 40

SANTIAGO, DR

Catalonia's house was always heavily guarded because of her son's status in the game. She hated to feel like she was on lockdown 24/7 but she respected her son's wishes.

At seventy-six years old, Catalonia still was able to walk around, cook, do yoga, and get her freak on. Luckily, doing yoga for over forty years had blessed her with a little grip left in her pussy.

She was baking muffins and carrot cake for one of the guard's birthday and she wanted to surprise him, plus, she had a little crush on him. She had always loved dark-skinned men ever since she'd been a young woman. With nine children, she'd always had that grandma-energy to show people her caring side. There was also a side to Catalonia that only few knew about—most would say her smile and loving energy was Catalonia's true self.

Being raised into the Dominican Cartel she'd had her fair share of killing and drug selling all over the world. She'd killed one of her daughters a while back because some money came up missing from a stash house in Santo Domingo. When Catalonia found out Venus and her husband had robbed her, she killed both of them and chopped off their hands.

The oven ticked letting her know one of the cakes was now done.

"Grandma," Pablo said, entering the kitchen with his handsome smile.

"Pablo, come give me a hug." Catalonia was more than happy to see her grandbaby.

"It smells good in here." Pablo took a seat as he stared at his grandma's tight leggings and shook his head.

"You're right on time," she said, speaking good English.

"I won't be staying long. I just came by to show you some love."

"Oh, that's sweet. How're things going out in Miami? I used to be big time out there. I bet they still remember me." She chuckled.

"It's okay. I can't complain."

"You sure?" She gave him a look of uncertainty.

"Business is never easy."

"I hear you got a new girlfriend." She smiled.

"How did you know?"

"I know a lot, Pablo, so cut the bullshit. Why are you here?" She turned around to see her grandson pointing a gun at her which made Catalonia laugh.

"You knew I was coming?"

"Yep."

"Danilo told you, huh?"

"Of course, he's my son, but I'm glad we can meet up like this now, because I have a confession." She took a deep breath.

"This gonna be good?" Pablo lowered his gun. When he arrived, the guards were all happy to see him because they had love for Pablo way more than Danilo who had told them to kill Pablo on sight. Yet that was out of the question because Pablo had always treated them good.

"I know you heard a lot of different stories about your mom and father's death growing up, but the truth is they both stole from me," Catalonia said.

"My mom never stole," he spat back, defending his mom.

"She did, and I killed her and your father, because he was the mastermind. When I tortured them it hurt me but Venus had to learn a lesson," his grandmom stated.

Pablo always knew his grandma was a serious person but he didn't think Catalonia would kill her own creation.

"I don't believe you."

"I will get nothing out of lying but I have a gift for you." She went to the cabinet and he watched her every move.

Catalonia pulled out two large jars and placed them on the table.

"What the fuck is that?" he shouted, seeing a bloody hand in both jars which were filled with water.

"This one is your mom's hand and the other one is your father's hand." His grandma was very calm.

Pablo saw his mom's wedding ring and he knew it was all true—everything she'd just told him.

Bloc! Bloc! Bloc! Bloc!

Catalonia's chest vibrated when the hollow tip bullets hit her heart and her body slowly collapsed onto the stove.

Pablo had tears in his eyes. He'd never met someone more vicious than his grandma. Seeing Catalonia die with her eyes wide open made him feel a bit better. He spit in her face then went outside.

"Y'all about to come work for me and it's about to be a war within our own family," he told the guards. They nodded letting the young boss know they had him.

Amora waited for him inside the car wondering what the fuck the loud noise inside had come from.

"You straight, baby?" she asked, as he got in the SUV with her in the back.

The truck pulled off going to Pablo's next location. He was headed to speak with another major king pen in the DR to find out if he could get him on the team. He'd come up with a smart idea to connect with all Danilo's enemies and join forces with them, promising them Danilo's drug turfs, and his life.

At first, he was gonna take Amora and run away, but that wasn't him. Pablo wanted to take care of his loose ends first then go somewhere far away.

"Everything fantastic, love. Enjoy the ride." He kissed her lips. Amora couldn't help but wonder what she'd gotten herself into.

PALM BEACH COUNTY, MIAMI

"YOU SURE THIS IS A GOOD IDEA because you know the long history we got with them niggas," Rush's friend Loc Dog said, pulling into the high school parking lot four cars deep.

Rush had set up a meeting with Lil Blood who ran the Bloods in Palm Beach. The two gangs had been beefing since the little niggas caused a little of bloodshed in the city.

Since Rush was now the plug in Palm Beach, he felt like instead of beefing, it was time to get money. There was a group of Bloods waiting for Rush and his crew.

"It's time, cuz." Rush got out and walked up to the crew who were all standing in a straight line with Lil Blood leading the pack.

"Rush, Loc, I've been hearing your name a lot lately in these streets, bruh." Lil Blood was dripping in designer gear. He was six-five and a vicious shooter in the street, with a long body count.

"I called you out so we can put the dumb shit behind us and focus on the bag," Rush said.

"That's real, homie. I heard how you did Big Hulu. I was copping work from him but if you hadn't killed him I would've." Lil Blood hated Big Hulu but he was his only secure drug supply.

"You got me now and my product is better and cheaper."

"I heard, bruh."

"So, you down?" Rush asked.

Lil Blood looked at his crew who were all about getting money and he knew he had to feed them and his family, and this was the only way.

"Facts, we locked in, bruh. All that beef shit behind us."

"Let's turn the city up then."

"I'm with you."

Rush and Lil Blood embraced and talked for a few minutes about future plans. Everything was falling into place and Rush had some people in Tampa who were already locking shit down out there for him.

CHAPTER 41

DOWNTOWN, MIAMI

"How did you people even know he was here at this hotel?" Lil BD asked Vina. as they did a steak out.

"I have a person close to me who came here and informed me that they'd seen Maloney and heard his accent. Look at the Sprinters parked over there." Vina pointed to the end of the hotel lot where two Sprinter vans were parked.

"Let's just run up in there. I'm not in the mood to wait," Lil BD said, running out of patience because he had a headache.

"You're acting real impertinent and impolite today," she told him, looking out of the Aston Martin windows. She needed to make sure her two truckloads of goons were still on point as they waited for Maloney to come out.

"I'm a little sorry I can't be gracious every day," he said.

"You're on a fuckin' roll today, so I'ma get you a tampon from CVS because you're getting blood on my seats," she said, hitting his pressure points. Before he could reply, Maloney and a crew of weird looking dudes dressed in robes came out with him.

"On the money," Lil BD said, slipping out with the Draco.

Vina tried to stop him so she could text her men, but Lil BD was already in the middle of the lot. She inched out of the car and followed her stubborn boyfriend.

Tat-Tat! Tat-Tat-Tat! Boc! Boc!

Lil BD hit two of the guards and Maloney ripped their bodies in half. Maloney moved fast, spinning around while firing at Lil BD who also got hit, but Vina helped him stagger in between cars.

"Are you stupid?" Vina asked, decking low between the car. Finally seeing her men get out the trucks, they began to open fire.

"I got it!" Lil BD popped back blasting the Draco, this time making Maloney run down the lot.

Vina saw Maloney and chased him while letting off her Glock. She hit him once. Two men almost had Vina in their targets until Lil BD put holes in their chests.

"Stay your ass put." Lil BD pulled Vina next to him on the side of the wall, near the hotel's front sliding doors.

Lil BD saw how Vina's crew took care of the rest of Maloney's men but he still got away. Vina started up the car and Lil BD jumped inside.

"He got away again," Vina said, disappointed.

"I would've had him."

"Oh yeah, that's what you think?" She laughed.

"I almost had him."

"Baby, please. You don't have to fake it for me. I just saved your ass for the third time, shit maybe the fourth. I lost count but aye who's counting." She smiled knowing how to crush his ego.

"Whatever."

"It's okay, baby, that's why I'm yours."

"I should've let them shoot your ass back there," Lil BD said. Vina laughed hard as she entered South Miami and crossed the bridge.

"Baby?"

"Yeah."

"Is it a good time to tell you I'm pregnant?" she asked, when she stopped behind traffic.

"You're pregnant?"

"I just said it, so yeah?" she replied.

"You wanna have a baby with me?" he asked, seriously.

"Yes, I do. These past couple of months with you have been the highlight of my life. I want to really have a family with you. Even on our bad days, like today, I value them, baby," she told him.

'I cherish you too and I'll be the best father ever." He kissed her lips then rubbed her stomach which was still flat.

"I know I would get pregnant quickly but you blow it off," she told him.

"Everything happens for a reason," he said feeling like his life was repeating itself. When his ex, Jenny, got pregnant before she was killed, he'd felt the same happiness but he swore to protect Vina with his own life.

NORTH MIAMI

CHLOE DANCED AROUND HER CONDO while picking up the rest of Hitler's shit so she could throw it out. When her boyfriend died she didn't shed one tear, seeing him pop up on the news, something in her gut told her the night before, something terrible had happened to him. Hitler was really starting to become a headache so someone taking him out of his misery had taken a load off her. Somehow Hitler reminded her of Animal, and as time went on, it became a big turn off.

The loud bang on her door made Chloe snatch her gun off the living room table. "Who the hell is it?" she yelled.

"Maloney!"

"Maloney, what the fuck are you doing here?" Chloe unlocked the door to let him inside and he rushed in.

"Shot me," he cried, growling in pain, while holding his back left shoulder.

"And you came here?"

"I had to." Maloney started to walk into her living room on her white rugs which she'd paid lots of money for.

"Oh no you don't! Take that shit into the kitchen," Chloe yelled, re-directing him to the kitchen sink area.

"Vina and Lil BD knew where I was staying and shot me." Maloney took off his shirt, showing his nice body.

"Wow, nice body." Chloe was impressed

"I need a first aid kit."

"I got alcohol and towels, plus the bullet went in and out, so you're good," Chloe said, stepping out to get him some items to clean his wound.

"I'ma kill both of them. I almost got killed," he spat, as she laughed.

"You look like a cute white Jamaican when you get mad. Them blue eyes turn red quick, papi. Cute." Chloe joked but it was clear he wasn't in the mood.

"This is no joking matter and I have to fly out to New York tomorrow," Maloney said, pulling out his phone to make some important calls.

"I'll come."

"No way."

"Yeah, I need to do some shopping up there anyway," Chloe said, as he went on her private terrace to make a call.

Since Hitler was gone, she needed another man to replace his company, and she looked at Maloney knowing he could do it.

SOUTH, MIAMI

ROWLEY HAD BEEN HIDING OUT at a close friend's apartment looking for the Haitian Mafia. In an hour, he was gonna shake up the city and get some answers for his wife's death.

Kamla tried to stop him from going out there but nothing could make him turn away, and just because Luc or Boss didn't feel any emotions, he did. Whatever Luc or Boss loved, he wanted to kill it so they could feel his pain. He dressed up in all-black and he strapped himself up with guns, knives, and a vest.

Liberty City and Lil Haiti were the Haitians grounds so those neighborhoods would be his first stop tonight, until someone told him what he wanted to hear. Rowley understood that what he was about to do was dangerous, but he had nothing to live for anymore.

CHAPTER 42

MANHATTAN, NY

Amora waited patiently inside a well-own bar and grill restaurant located near 42nd St.. This would be her first time face to face with her father, and she was feeling all types of different emotions.

Pablo came to New York with her and he knew a lot of people in the Bronx and Washington Heights area so he was running around out there. Her aunty told Amora earlier, that her father had come by and requested to meet up with his daughter days ago. Hearing that, she shot up to New York and set up tonight's meeting. She looked cute in a dress and heels with her hair done up in a bun with Chinese bangs.

The establishment was filled tonight and Amore had no clue what her dad even looked like. While staring at the menu, she just so happened to leave her table and saw a White man standing in front of her table staring.

"Excuse me, can I help you?" she asked.

"Amoro?" he replied.

"Yes, who are you?" She looked into his blue eyes and felt awkward because he'd ended up tearing up.

"I'm Maloney, your father."

"You must have the wrong person. I'm black." Amora always knew she was mixed with something but she had still considered herself a Black woman. Growing up, kids at school used to pick on her because of the color of her skin and she used to wish her skin was darker so people wouldn't bully her. Eventually, she had learned how to live with who she was.

"Your mother, Savannah McCorner, recently passed, and before that, we were supposed to set this up, but I lost contact and eventually got in touch with a woman who is your aunt." Maloney stood there and noticed her expression change.

Everything he'd just said was true but Amora still couldn't wrap her fingers around how she had a White dad.

"Sit down. I'm just overwhelmed because I always thought my dad was Black."

"I'm Black, Amora. I'm Caribbean, but some people from the island look just like me or you. I'm just so sorry it took this long to come to see you. When I heard of you, I couldn't believe it, and I was upset at your mother for not telling me sooner because I would have been there for you," Maloney told her.

"I don't want to go into the past. I understand, and my mom told me it was a one-night-stand type thing."

"You're beautiful."

"Thanks. You look younger than I would've imagined," she said, looking at his youthful face and long dreads.

"I eat and train good."

"That's cool."

"I heard you were in college," Maloney said, ready to eat.

"Yeah, but I rather not talk about it," she admitted.

"If I can be of help let me know."

"What do you do for a living?" She looked at his fancy suit.

"I won't build the relationship off lies and you're grown so I'm going to be honest with you. I run a drug trafficking organization in the Caribbean," he said.

Amora felt like everybody she was meeting was a criminal or some type of Kingpin drug dealer.

'I don't judge."

"How long will you be out here? I have some business to attend down south and I'm trying to handle it then I'll be able to get a condo out here. We can spend time and catch up if that's what you want," he told her.

"Why not? But at the moment. I'm moving around myself, so you just have to catch me at the right time."

"Well, let's eat for now. Do they have Caribbean food here?" 'Maloney asked, making her laugh.

"I don't know." Amora now knew where she got her exotics looks from.

SOUTH MIAMI

Boss came out to Carol City so he could holla at Luc. Luc had texted him and told him to meet him at a low-key apartment where they'd hide weapons.

Walking up the stairs, he was on the phone with Lil BD who he hadn't seen in a few weeks.

"Yo', I almost killed that nigga!" Lil BD shouted on the Facetime call, talking about the shootout they'd had with Maloney.

"He ain't on shit anyway," Boss replied.

"Man, that nigga be rollin' with ninjas or some power rangers. What the fuck you mean he not on shit?"

"That be for show, bro, but where are you at anyway? Mom asked about you last week," Boss told him.

"Laying low. Vina pregnant."

"What? I'm about to be an uncle and you just now telling me, goofy nigga?" Boss joked, happy to hear the news. He looked at Lil BD's smile on the screen and knew his little brother was more than excited.

"I'm blessed, bro. Vina is the one. She a crazy, Spanish bitch, but her love is from the heart not the mouth."

"That's real but let me hit you back later. I'm 'bout to check Luc," Boss said.

"Fuck that nigga," Lil BD stated.

"Nah, he family."

"Yeah, but he be having bitch ways," Lil BD stated.

"You crazy." Boss hung up and stepped inside to see Luc inside drinking. He looked stressed with his sunglasses on.

"You good, bro?" Boss asked, looking at the half-empty bottle of cheap rum.

"Rowley went on a fuckin' killing spree last night and killed eight of our main workers and lit three of our trap houses on fire— we lost millions. That shit all over the fuckin' news," Luc stated.

"How is that possible?" Boss looked confused and made Luc laugh.

"Kamla and Rowley are not to be slept on. They dangerous people, Boss. I just spoke to Kamla and she said he was out here, but I

let my better half look past him and now it's biting me in the ass."
Luc took a gulp of liquor and felt its burn in his chest.

We gonna be straight."

"Can I trust you?"

"Of course," Boss replied.

"No, this is bigger than any of us could ever imagine, so before
I let you know what it is, I need to know if I can really trust you,"
Luc said, taking off his shades to look into Boss' eyes.

"You can trust me, Unc."

"Read this. Francisque left it for my eyes only but I can trust
you, I see," Luc said, handing him the letter.

Boss read the letter and his eyes widened as he read the con-
tents. When he'd finished it, he was full of rage, upset, disappointed,
and hurt all in one.

"Wow." he said.

"I know."

"Now what?"

"To be honest I haven't puzzled this crazy shit together yet."
Luc shook his head.

"Grandpa left us with the shit," Boss stated.

"He had his ways but he always spoke the truth."

"I'll never doubt that but this is really too much. How do we
even confront shit like this. Boss was lost.

"We don't, I guess. You wait for it to confront you," Luc added.

"This shit can ruin us."

"Yep."

"We gotta do something."

"Pray," Luc said, getting up to leave.

Boss stood there looking at the door shut and he slapped Luc's
bottle off the countertop.

CHAPTER 43

PALM BEACH COUNTY, MIAMI

Rush and Lil Blood shut down the club for Lil Blood birthday. They were turned up and had all the love the city could give. Dancers from Dade County, ATL, NYC, and D.C. had come out tonight and they weren't let down because the two crews were full of real ballers. There were so much ice in the club, it looked like a lighthouse in that bitch.

"I'm glad you came out, bruh," Lil Blood told Rush, as he watched two dancers sniff a line of coke off each other's nipples.

"This family now, bruh, you feel me? We came a long way at a young age, bruh." Rush popped a bottle of Moët.

"I been hearin' things, bruh, and I feel like I need to bring it to your attention," Lil Blood stated.

"Right now?" Rush was already having a hard time hearing in the club.

"Yeah? Hold up ... Y'all hoes step up out of here," Lil Blood told the dancers who were kissing each other.

"Okay, daddy," the women said, high as a kite.

"I been hearing you dealin' wit' some serious people," Lil Blood said.

"That's the word on the streets already?" Rush laughed.

"Yeah, but whatever you're into, I'm in now, so I just like to know what I'm dealing with in case shit ever goes left." Lil Blood made a clear point. He knew a lot of niggas who would meet plugs and get rich then months late they would pop up dead.

"You really wanna know, bruh?" Rush took a sip from the bottle

"I wouldn't had asked if I didn't. Believe dat, bruh."

"I'm down with the Haitian Mafia," Rush said. Lil Blood started laughing so hard vomit almost came out of his nose.

"Nah, bro, for real, all jokes aside," Lil Blood stated.

Mostly everybody in the tri-counties which were Broward County, Palm Beach County, and Dade County knew who the Haitian Mafia was and how they got down.

To be a part of them, Lil Blood knew a nigga had to be family, and nobody fucked with them, not even the Cartels.

"I'm really Haitian Mafia, bruh, and that's who you work for now."

"Lil Blood saw how serious Rush was and stopped laughing.

"You serious?"

"Hell yeah! We about to be rich."

"Oh shit, this is big!"

"Keep that between us, cuz, you feel me?" Rush made clear because he didn't want his business in the street.

"Say less, bruh."

"Let's finish this party 'cause I'm 'bout to take me two or three women home."

"Me too, bruh." Lil Blood saw six dancers walking around sack chasing so he called them in their section.

DOWNTOWN, CHI'RAQ

Two Months Later ...

THE AIRPORT WAS HAVING A LOT of flight delays due to heavy winds. Boss was stuck with hundreds of people going through the same frustration. He sat down wishing he would've rented a private jet. However, he didn't have much because he had to rush to Chi-Town to make sure Juball's load landed on time.

The sit down he had with Juball went well and he'd gotten every top gang leader on board for what Boss had in mind.

Boss didn't know what to do or who to trust, but he did know some shit was about to hit the fan and cause a lot of blood. As the effects of the beef and tea he'd made caused his stomach to boil, Boss got up and headed to the restroom to take a shit.

His flight still had four hours before takeoff time if the winds slowed down, but in the Mid-West, high winds were regular and there were flight delays all the time.

The restroom was clean unlike most airports. Shutting the stall door, Boss took one of the best number two he'd had in a while.

182

After flushing and wiping his ass, it was time to go. While washing his hands, a man wearing a hat and sunglasses entered and locked the door.

Boss didn't have a gun because airport security was thick and on it, but he did have a pocketknife he pulled out quickly.

"Boss, I come in peace. No need for the knife," the man said, taking off his sunglasses and hat.

"Pablo, I should butcher your young ass." Boss got pissed.

"Hold on, calm down. I know this is awkward but I'm not wit' Danilo no more and I can be a better help than enemy to you. I'm not on any type of sneaky snake shit," Pablo made clear, hoping Boss would.

"Just because you don't work for your uncle don't mean we can be cool," Boss told him.

"I need your help."

"*My help?* That won't happen."

"I'm trying to kill Danilo. I just killed his mother."

"Hold up, you killed your own grandma?" Boss couldn't help but laugh.

"Yeah."

"Danilo gonna bury you alive."

"He might but I just gotta get him first, bro," Pablo said.

"What do you need me for?"

"I wanna take over the DR cartel once I kill Danilo. I'ma need a plug, Boss." Pablo saw Boss' facial expression change as if he was thinking.

"Okay, get rid of Danilo and your girlfriend and I'll see what I can do," Boss said, getting a paper towel to wipe his hands.

"*My girlfriend?* What does she have to do with this?"

"Oh, you don't know?" Boss asked, seeing Pablo clearly didn't know who he was fuckin'.

"I did my research on Maloney to find out if he had any family I could kill. I recently found out Maloney's name was mentioned in a dead person's will along with his daughter, Amora. I then had my people look for her and she was somewhere with you," Boss said, just as people began to knock on the bathroom door.

"She's green to this, Boss."

"If you can find a way to get her to bring me Maloney, then I'll leave her alone and I'll supply you," Boss said, before leaving him in the restroom. A group of civilians rushed the restroom. They needed to piss and some were upset because they'd been made to wait and hold it while outside waiting.

COSTA RICA

Three Months Later ...

Vina was six months pregnant but would be seven in two weeks—her tummy was showing big time. Her face, feet, and body had blown up like an air balloon, but she didn't care one bit. Her and Lil BD lay in bed watching Love and Hip-Hop on TV.

So far, her pregnancy had been healthy and Lil BD had been there for her day and night. He'd let the boss control everything while he helped Vina manage her Cartel. He had no clue she was a billionaire. Every day, she had Lil BD ship out coke and heroin all over the world. She was making ten times more money than his family and he couldn't believe it because of her young age.

Vina wanted to deliver her baby boy in her country and Lil BD was fine with that since he was more hyped than she was. He could hardly wait to welcome his new seed to the world.

CHAPTER 44

MIAMI BEACH, MIAMI

Kristian rushed home from school after she'd got the call letting her know that her father wasn't feeling well. During the entire ride home, she prayed he would be okay because losing another family member would break her little heart.

When she'd received the news of how her grandma died, she couldn't believe it. Knowing that there were people in the world with no conscious or emotion made her scared.

Pulling into the driveway, she realized the place was filled with security men but more than normal.

"Where's papi?" she asked one of the guards who had been on her father's crew of elite goons for years.

" He's inside, upstairs in his room. But before you go, I need to let you know it's bad, but we gotta have faith," the guard told her, making Kristina a little nervous.

"What the hell are you talking about?" she asked.

"He didn't tell you?" the guard asked with a solemn look on his face. "I'm sorry, just go on inside. The doctors are up there with him and they'll explain everything," the man told her.

"*Doctors*?" Kristina repeated to herself before turning to take off running up the stairs like a track star.

Kristina stormed in the master bedroom without knocking, scaring the two nurses who surrounded Danilo. He looked deathly ill. When she had stopped by two weeks ago he appeared to be just fine, now he looked like he'd lost one hundred pounds overnight.

"Papi, what happened?" She rushed to his bedside and reached for his frail, cold hand.

"I'm sorry, baby." His voice was low and raspy.

"For what? Why are these IVs hooked up to you?" she asked.

'I'm dying, sweetheart," he said just above a whisper, "I have cancer, and I could die any day."

"What? Nooo, Papi, no!" she cried, "you can't leave me!"

"It's okay, baby. I love you but I need to ask you a favor," Danilo asked. The nurses left the room to give them some alone time and privacy.

'I'll do anything for you, Papi."

"Pablo is no longer part of the family," he began, "he's an enemy, and there is only one person left to take over the family business since your sister is gone."

"Who? Me, Papi?" Kristina asked, with eyes wide open.

"Yes, and you have to control it and guard it with your whole heart. Your family in the DR will show you the things you need to know. I've already informed them and given them orders," Danilo said, taking a deep breath.

"I don't know how to run a Cartel."

"Yes you do, baby. The main thing you need to do is handle the business at hand," he told her.

"What's that?"

"You've had the brains to figure things out since you were a little girl. You're smarter than any child I've ever known."

"I have to kill Pablo?" she asked.

"Yes, or he will kill you just like he killed your grandmother," Danilo told her.

'He killed granny?" Kristina had fire in her eyes.

"Yes."

"Papi, you can beat the cancer," she said, "I've seen you win bigger battles. Fight, Papi," she pleaded, though it was out of his hands.

"No, baby, it's too late and the cancer has already spread. I've had it for eight months now but didn't want to tell you," he said sadly.

"But why?" she whined. "I've always feared the time when you would have to leave me, but I'm not going anywhere." She held his hand and sat with him. Her mind was heavy and clouded with thoughts of how she would be able to run a Cartel.

PORT OF SPAIN, TRINIDAD

Rowley had gone back to pick up some bombs from an island man he'd known for years. The man had access to any type of bomb known to mankind.

Two nights prior, Rowley had got a lead on Boss' location and he had plans to bomb his car, house, and anyone close to him.

***

Rowley's face was displayed all over the world news because he'd left DNA at the crime scene and now he was a wanted man.

The man who made the bombs lived on the island in the poverty section of the city, in a small shed.

"DH, it's me," Rowley yelled.

A bald head man peeped his head out and told him to come inside. Rowley saw a bunch of metal, bombs, chemical containers, and devices.

"Is the tool ready?" He spoke in code because DH was a nervous wreck after doing fifteen years in prison for selling bombs in the UK.

"I have to go to the back and get it; give me one second. The man rushed out and Rowley shook his head thinking about which one of his boats he was going to use so he could head back to Miami.

After waiting only a few seconds and looking around at all of DH's crazy shit, the door slowly opened.

"Come on, DH, I have to— Rowley paused when he saw his sister walk into the shed holding the biggest handgun he'd ever seen in his life.

"You don't listen, Rowley."

"Kamla, put the gun down. What are you doing?"

"I know what you're about to do and I'm sorry but I can't let you," Kamla told him.

He gave her a sly smirk. "You can't stop what I'm about to do, Kamla. The Haitians have been causing grief in our lives and you just let it happen," he scolded her.

"This shit is about to be bigger than me and you both."

"No, I know what it is… you still got Luc's dick in your mouth, bitch!"

Bloc! Bloc!

Kamla hit him in the shoulder twice and he cried in pain and knelt down on one knee.

"Like I was trying to say, you led your wars, Rowley, but it's about power, and strength comes from power. In this game, you have to do anything and everything to get power. We are the Mafia, and we live by values, but we don't believe in morals because certain morals will get you killed. I value my guns and money for the distance in between," she said as he bleed profusely.

"Fuck you, snake bitch! Somebody gonna kill you and I hope it be Luc or the Tobaga Mafia!" Rowley yelled and put pressure on his shoulder— the blood wouldn't stop.

"Luc and I have a clear understanding, Rowley, and he will always be my living husband. Who do you think we've been getting our dope from all these fuckin' years? Jesus or fuckin' El Chapo."

Luc had been supplying his wife ever since they were married, and even though they fell out, he still made sure he sent her orders every week; however, no one knew except the two of them.

"Fuck you, Kamla!"

"I gotta run, brotha. At least you can join your wife."

"Kamla, Kamla, Kamla!"

Bloc! Bloc! Bloc-Bloc!

Rowley's body hit the ground knocking over the acid which then spilled all over his skin. Kamla watched as his skin peeled and shed from Rowley's face.

"Damn, I gotta get me some of that shit," she told herself out loud, as DH walked back inside.

DH had called Kamla and told her Rowley was looking for bombs and acting very strange, so she rushed down.

"Clean this shit up," she told the creepy, old man.

"Is he dead?" DH asked.

"Better yet shoot him."

Bloc! Bloc! Bloc!

Kamla shot him in the head then went home.

SANTIAGO, DOMINICAN REPUBLIC

Two Weeks Later ...

KRISTINA HAD TEARS ALL over her black dress as the priest spoke in Spanish. She had given her dad the proper funeral he deserved back home in the DR.

Three days after Danilo had told her he had cancer, he'd died in his sleep. When she woke up in her room that morning, she felt there were something wrong.

Close to six hundred people came out to show respect. She was guarded with over fifty-plus men, ready to kill for the new Cartel boss. During the funeral, Kristina sat at the front of the church her father had grown up in but something was really bothering her.

Now that the funeral was over, she stood up and made her way through the crowd to where Pablo and a gang of his men had been during the duration of the service.

"You must've been too nervous to show your fuckin' face," Kristina told Pablo with a smirk.

"I see Danilo already put the bug in your ear before I got a chance to come talk to you," Pablo shot back.

"Pablo, we're gonna put the past in the past. Please, just let my dad rest in peace," she said.

"Fair. I was just leaving. And congratulations on your new position. It's a big one but I'm sure you can handle it." Pablo walked off.

"I want you to make the call," Kristina told one of her guards who had been watching Pablo leave with his twenty goons, all dressed in black.

Romell Tukes

CHAPTER 45

NORWOOD, MIAMI

It was early morning and Boss walked out of his apartment to see a small note on his Rolls Royce Wraith windshield. The letter read: *Miami Dade County Zoo at 11 a.m.. and come alone or there will be issues for you…*

Boss read the letter over ten times, and the fucked up handwriting looked so familiar, he figured out who it was from.   The following week he had to fly out to Costa Rica for Lil BD so he could be there for his nephew's birth. Boss was happy for Lil BD, not only because he was about to enter fatherhood, but mainly because of his fast growth. The other night they'd had a deep conversation about him leaving the game alone and being a family man.

Checking the Richard Muller on his left wrist, he knew it was then minutes before 11 a.m., and luckily, he lived minutes away from the zoo. Driving to the zoo, Boss thought about the letter Luc had let him read and still couldn't get it out his head. Things were starting to go well on the business side and his plans for Chicago were also coming together.

When he made it to the Dade County Zoo, he checked his surroundings to make sure it wasn't a setup. Once he placed his gun on his hip, he looked for a certain location to meet the mysterious person, but to his surprise, there wasn't one. He walked around looking at the wild animals and his favorite Lions roaring and scaring kids.

"Boss," a woman whispered from behind him. He turned around to see a woman dressed in a disguised outfit.

"Lexus?" he said, at the sound her voice.

"Shhhh … Come sit down." She moved a bag while drinking coffee and watching animals.

"Why are you wearing all dat shit, Lexus, and what the fuck is going on? We not cool. I still want to put a bullet in your fuckin' face," Boss made clear.

"Shut up and look at the little kid in the blue sweatsuit with the long hair." Lexus pointed to him.

Boss saw the little kid holding a lady's hand as she showed him the different animals. When Boss saw the look on the kid's face he felt like he was looking at a mini version of himself.

"Oh my God.. you wasn't lying." 'Boss couldn't believe it.

"I would never lie to you I'm not you, Boss."

"Can I meet him?"

"Not right now. I just wanted to let you know we have a kid," Lexus told him.

"Thank you."

"No problem, but I have to go."

"How did you know where I lived anyway? Not even my brother knows. "

"I know a lot, Boss. You're forgetting who I am."

"Where do we go from here, Lexus?"

"I don't know, and only time will tell because I may still have to kill you one day. I don't trust you," she stated. She stood up and dropped a note in his lap.

"I should be the only one you trust," he replied.

"You crossed that line when you let your people kill my father." She walked off to play with her son and show him around the zoo.

Boss looked at the note and it had an address on it but the other side read: *Chloe is following you...*

Damn it, little bitch, he thought to himself. He wondered how he had let her catch up to him. He chose to play it smart and play dumb at the same time. Since she was already following him, he put a little plan together.

NORTH MIAMI, FL

CHLOE TOOK THE ELEVATOR to her condo after a long day of stalking Boss. She could have killed Boss plenty of times but she'd concluded he could be more useful alive instead of dead. She was having a little fun watching his every move, especially when he went to the gym to work out and reveal those sexy muscles. Now Boss had gone home for the night so she stopped at a Waffle house to get a bite to eat. Afterwards, she'd headed home.

Walking inside her condo she thought about texting him to see if he was still in the Bahamas taking care of his business.

Whack! A lamp came smashing down on the back of her head.

"Ahh," she growled on the floor, bleeding and becoming light-headed and dizzy.

"Bitch, get the fuck up!" Boss said, as he grabbed her by the long ponytail she was styling.

"Wait," she cried, before he flung her into the wall, busting her nose and lips.

"This whole time, you really thought you wouldn't run in to me, Chloe, huh?" Boss had a crazy look in his eyes as he kneeled down in front of her.

"I'm sorry, Boss, but I need you to hear me out." As she talked, she coughed up blood and prayed he wouldn't abuse her anymore.

"Chloe, are you sane?"

"I want you to fuck me." Her words made Boss smile.

"Bitch, I wouldn't dare stick a finger in you."

"One time," she begged as she looked over his shoulder.

Click!— a gun cocked behind Boss.

"Don't move, Boss," a voice said.

"I see what's going on," Boss said, putting his hand in the air. He turned around and came face to face with Louis. Louis had crept inside the condo to surprise Chloe.

"Thank you, Louis. This fool was about to rape me," Chloe stated, slowly getting up from the floor.

"I been waiting for this day," Louis said.

"Well, don't waste it on talkin'," Boss suggested.

"Let's torture him. I got some good shit in the room that I keep for special occasions," Chloe said, standing by Louis like he was her boo.

"Go get it and hurry back," Louis told her. He was ready to have some fun.

"You crossed your own family. How do you feel about that?" Boss questioned him.

"Fuck all of you clowns! I'ma kill all you bitches off!"

Boom! Boom! Boom!

Boss ducked when he saw Louis' head bust wide open. Lil BD appeared in all-black clothing and he had an extra-large gun in his hand.

"Oh shit! When you get here?" Boss asked, happy to see him.

"I saved your ass but you need to thank Vina." Lil BD had handed Boss the other gun right on time.

"I thought you was gonna wait me to come," Chloe said, coming out with a bag full of tools. When she'd heard the gun fire she assumed Louis had killed Boss and not the other way around. Her plan to have fun had just been ruined.

"Surprise!" Boss said, pointing the gun at her face.

Chloe looked at Louis on the floor with his head blown off then her eyes went to Lil BD and Boss. She knew it was over for her.

"Shit," she mumbled.

"Yeah, bitch, you fucked up," Lil BD said.

"I really fuckin' hate the both of you!" Chloe poked her lip out.

"We hate you too, bitch, but you did put up a fight." Boss kept it real.

"I did my best," she admitted.

"Not enough," Boss could tell she wanted to try her hand so he saved her the trouble.

Boc-Boc! Boc! Boc! Her body was loaded with bullets from Lil BD's and Boss' weapon before they walked out. It landed right next to Louis's.

CHAPTER 46

MIAMI UNIVERSITY, MIAMI

Amora had gone out to her school to pick up some things she'd left inside her dorm room. Pablo didn't want her to leave the new apartment they'd got together, so she'd snuck out when he was asleep. She did, however, leave him with a note. He'd been very overprotected and he'd been acting strangely lately.

Amora didn't know what was going on because Pablo hadn't told her much except that there was a war was going on. She had to leave college and be a homebody which was something she'd feared at her young age.

Meeting her father a few months back was too much pressure to deal with and still have to deal with Pablo's issues. She had really been thinking about re-considering her relationship with Pablo.

Every Night since meeting Maloney, they would talk on the phone for hours. He was super cool and they had been heavily building their father-daughter relationship. Maloney had even sent her a birthday gift the week before—a new Porsche Coupe that she loved so much.

Walking into her college dorm felt good and she missed being in college. She missed studying, the classes, the parties, and the other college kids.

She dug into her purse to get her dorm room key and found it with ease. Her roommate normally worked on Thursdays so she'd have plenty of time to pack up whatever she needed.

The inside of the dorm room was the same way she'd left it. She grabbed her gym bag and put her laptop and a few other things in the bag so could use it at the home and instead of being stuck inside struck with boredom.

After packing everything up she headed to the door and opened it, and to her surprise, Kristina was standing right there.

'Oh my God, Kristina, you scared the hell outta me!" Amora held her heart, breathing heavily.

"Amora." Kristina had a devilish tone to her voice.

"You okay?" Amora could tell something was very wrong with Kristina.

"How've you been?"

"Great! Have you been in school?"

"Amora cut the small talk and got straight to the point. Bitch, you still with Pablo?"

"Kristina, what's up with you?"

"*Me?* Bitch, I ain't do shit to you so you have no reason coming up here talking all spicy and shit," she said, standing close to Amora's face.

"Okay, calm down, Kristina, and let's just talk about this real quick. I'm sure we can talk about it," Amora pleaded.

"Shut the fuck up and sit down," she told Amora, who, by now, was sweating bullets.

"I'm sorry for whatever I've done to you. We're friends."

"For one, bitch, we were never friends! You're a stuck-up hoe from New York who thinks you're better than everybody else!" Kristina shouted.

"Your cousin likes it and you sound jealous." Amora couldn't help her outburst, even with a gun to her head.

"Pablo is the reason you're her right now."

"What?" Amora was confused.

"Pablo killed my grandma and since I took over my family business, he has to go! So since I see you two getting real cozy, I'ma kill you first!"

"I hate evil bitches like you," Amora said, kicking Kristina in her private part then jumping up as she bent over from the pain in her ribs.

Amora attacked which caused the gun to fall to the floor, and they wrestled and fought while rolling around all over the floor. She punched Kristina in the face twice before Kristina caught her with a clean elbow to the face.

"Bitch!" Amora yelled, right before giving Kristina a hard kick to her chest. Then, she reached for the gun which was now within arm's reach.

Kristian grabbed Amora's ankles when she realized she was going for the gun. Amora fell on the floor and Kristina started banging her head into the floor over and over.

Amora's body became lifeless and Kristina got up and snatched up her gun.

Boc! Boc! Boc! Amora lay dead inches away from her ringing iPhone. Seeing Pablo's face pop up on the screen, Kristina answered it.

"Cousin," she answered breathlessly.

"Where is she, Kristina?"

"It seems that my Amora is taking a permanent nap," she replied.

"Don't fuckin' play with me, you little bitch! Where is she?" Pablo screamed.

"Calm down, playa, I just told your dumb ass she's dead. Now let the games begin, cousin. Bye-bye," Kristina said and hung up. Stepping over Amora's body, she exited the room.

"I need to get back in the damn gym," she said to herself as she hurried down the hall.

She'd known Amora would be coming back to school soon to withdraw or clean her dorm room, so Kristina had stuck around and told the students in Amora's dorm to call when she arrived. She knew it would make Pablo angry and push him to his breaking point but she had big plans for him.

UNIVERSITY HOSPITAL, MIAMI

Vina was in the hospital giving birth to her son and everybody was out there, from Luc, Boss, Janella, and a gang of security guards patrolling the hospital as if they were the national guardsmen. Lil BD was the only one in the room while she was giving birth because the hospital only allowed one person in the room at a time.

"I got a grandbaby now," Janella said, as she tied her dreads together.

***

"That just means you're getting old, sis." Luc started laughing.

"Boy, I look younger than both of you," Janella said, standing outside the hospital room.

"Y'all crazy." Boss looked in the room and saw Vina still pushing.

"I can't believe Louis is finally dead. I hope that nigga don't pop back up." Luc gave Boss a look.

Once Luc got the news about how they had killed Chloe and Louis, he couldn't believe their two main problems were had finally been eliminated.

"Nah, he's dead, trust me," Boss said, "if it wasn't for Vina making the choice to give birth in Miami, it would've been me dead instead," he added seriously.

"How did you find out where she lived? Lord knows I've been trying to kill that hoe forever," Janella asked.

"Lexus gave me her info."

"*Lexus?*" Janella and Luc replied at the same time.

Boss hadn't told anyone he had a child with Lexus yet because it wasn't the place or time. "I found the info in my mailbox and it was kind of weird," he lied.

"You need to move then," Luc added, just when he realized Vina had delivered the baby. She waved them all inside.

"I named him Francisque," Lil BD told them.

"Why would you do that?" Luc asked.

"To let our grandfather's name live on," Lil BD stated.

"Me and Lil BD are moving to Miami," Vina said. Nearly everyone in the room had a surprised look on their face.

"That's good. Now we can be one big happy family," Janella said, embracing her grown-up grandbabies.

CHAPTER 47

WESTSIDE, CHI'RAQ

One Month Later ...

Juball's mind had been racing for the past hour. He'd received some terrible news about three of his traps. He called an emergency meeting with his main crew to find out what the fuck was going on.

Boss was sending Juball loads of keys twice a month on eighteen-wheelers driven by Juball's people because they owned a trucking company.

Having the eighteen-wheelers make trips to Miami and Chicago was easy, and it made shipping smooth for both parties.

Juball was already supplying most of the city and had formed allies with more gangstas than a few. The main gang in the city. the Latin Kings, weren't feeling Juball's new era of Chi'Raq Gangstas. A while back, they'd had a long war with Boss and his crew. The Gangsta Disciples, Vice Lords, Black P. Stones, and the Black Disciples were all fuckin' with Juball and the new Chi'Raq Gangstas movement.

One thing Juball knew about his city was that when it came to getting money, it didn't matter what color, race, gang, or hood you was from, everybody and anybody, would come together. He knew if someone had really robbed all three of his traps, shit would be all bad and he'd open all that stuff to Boss which could lead to a big problems. Juball didn't usually cross people when it came to his business affairs because he lived by the motto: *"treat people good, you never know when you would need them"*.

It was dark out when Juball arrived at the park and saw two of his cousins there. They were the same two cousins he'd he let control the stash houses and bag up the product for the streets.

Rushing out of the truck walking through Humboldt Park, the look on his cousin's face said enough. "We got robbed," Yayo said.

"How the fuck that shit happen?" He looked at Yayo and Dee-Dee, two Puerto Ricans from the Westside, and each man was about his bag. "I just got back and I heard what happened, P-Dub," Dee-Dee said using the P-Dub slang.

"I was on the Southside dropping off work to the Vice Lords before I headed over to my sister's crib for the evening. I made sure the stash houses were locked and straight before I slid," Yayo said.

"How the hell could somebody hit all three spots in one night?" Juball asked. He looked from one man to the other.

"Some youngin' told me he saw a bitch with red hair sticking out of her hoodie leaving the spot on TW Street. Then some old nigga my pops know said the same thing about the spot on LW Street—a red-headed bitch left the building with three bags," Yayo admitted.

"You tellin' me we got robbed by a bitch with red hair?" Juball felt himself about to explode in anger.

"I'm thinkin' it's the Latin Kings, bro. They been talkin' a lot of shit," DeeDee added.

"DeeDee you was outta town right?"

"Yeah," DeeDee replied.

"Since when you like to go outta town? And now all of sudden my spots been hit," Juball said.

"What you sayin', P-Dub? I had to go out to Iowa," DeeDee said defensively.

"You came back real fast, and the crazy part is, I saw you on social media three hours ago at club VIP," Juball said, pulling out his gun before aiming it at DeeDee's face.

DeeDee looked dumbfounded because he'd forgot about the post he'd put up in the club. He'd never been too bright and Juball knew off the rips something wasn't right when he started talking.

"Juball, I don't think the bro would cross us like that, P-Dub." Yayo looked at DeeDee

"Okay, man I'll explain. I fucked up. The bitch came at me with $200,000 in cash, bro. I let my greed take over my loyalty," DeeDee admitted. Yayo couldn't believe it. At that point, he even pulled his gun out and aimed at DeeDee.

"Who is the bitch?" Juball needed every detail.

"She had bunch of niggas with her when they ambushed me. And I didn't have no other options so I had to give up the spot. I'm sorry." DeeDee started to cry.

Boc! Boc-Boc! Boc! Boc-Boc!

"I want you to find out who this red-head bitch is and bring her to me alive. And leave this fuck nigga here," Juball told Yayo and walked off.

Juball knew Yayo would never cross him because he'd been loyal from the sandbox but DeeDee was always questionable. If he didn't find this red-head chick and get his shit back, he would have to start from the bottom, but worst of all, face Boss.

PORT AU PRINCE, HAITI

Luc sneaked inside the private mansion Janella secretly owned and nobody else knew about it. The week before he had followed her, and since then he'd been watching it closely.

That morning, Janella had told him she had to fly out to Miami for a few days, and it was the perfect time to search her crib.

The letter his father had left him exposed a lot of secrets, but the biggest of them all was Janella's second life.

Upstairs, Luc searched in the master bedroom under the bed, dressers, and inside the bookshelves for any documentaries concerning Janella. He looked inside the walk-in closet filled with heels and designer bags, trying to think where she would hide important papers. Then it popped in his head— her private gym. He knew she had one installed in every house she owned.

"Welcome, Luc," Janella said, surprising him when he turned to exit.

"Janella, I was just checking to see if you were here. Luc looked into the barrel of her gun.

"Cut the bullshit, Luc." Janella looked at a letter sticking out of his front shirt pocket that he'd forgot was there.

"You can put the gun down," Luc told her. She wasn't backing off whatsoever. He had left his gun in the jeep outside because he'd planned to be in and out.

'I'll take this." She snatched the letter out of his pocket. She began reading the letter from Francisque out loud. It was addressed to Luc...

Dear, My Son...

I'm sorry for what I'm about to tell you, but it's time you know something. First off, I have another daughter in the states. She is around Boss' age. I need you to look after her, please. I've named her Skylar. Janella has been working with the Haiti Government for years trying to destroy our family. She tried to have me and all of you assassinated twice, but my men killed the triggerman twice. I left her the family business because you wasn't ready. But by the time you receive this, I'm sure you will be. If Janella and takes over the Haitian Mafia, you may have to go to war with the Haiti government, who she works for. I'm sorry. I should've of told you sooner, My Son.

Love you ...

"Wow, that was harsh, he made me look really bad," Janella said.

"So it's all true?" Luc asked.

"Well yeah. When have you known daddy to be a liar?"

"Why we are all family and looked out for each other."

"Luc, I deserve more. I'm a boss not a worker when I lived in Chicago. Do you really think I was relaxing? No, I supplied other families, mainly all of dad's enemies, because I hated that nigga. Daddy having another child is new to me but I'll find her and kill her. I got some help now." Janella smiled.

"You really crazy."

"Thanks, but who else knows about this letter?" she asked.

"What does it matter? What's done in the dark is always brought out into the light," he said.

"I hate to be the bearer of bad news but this will be your last step," she said before pulling the trigger which was aimed at his chest.

Boc! Boc! Boc!

Luc's body hit the carpet and she ran out to see if Boss was still at the house preparing things for his next shipment.

Janella worried who else knew about the letter because it could do a lot of damage. She wouldn't let her cover be blown because everything was starting to fall in place. Her plan was simple—use the Haiti government to take over their island and use her children to control the money and drugs coming in and out of the states.

Luc would of become a big problem for her if she hadn't shot him, plus, she disliked him anyway.

LA FERRIERE, HAITI

BOSS POURED HIMSELF A DRINK after preparing his shipment for Miami. He looked at a recent missed call from Luc because his phone was on silent. But just as he was about to call him back, Janella rushed inside with a crazy look on her face.

"Hey, baby, is everything ready for tomorrow?" she asked him, sweating from her forehead.

"Yeah, you straight?"

"Yep, I was out exercising," she lied.

"In jeans and boots?"

"Muhammad Ali use to do it," Janella shot back.

"Okay, sure."

"Come with me to the guest house I have to show you something," Janella stated walking out of the front door. Boss followed with a cup in his hand.

The guest house was positioned on the side of the house and Janella spent most of her time there.

"You want a drink?" She went to the bar area and grabbed some stuff out of the cabinets.

"This should be good. I gotta catch this flight back to— Boss paused when he saw Janella pull out a gun from a hidden location.

"Did you read the letter?" Her words were cold and straight to the point.

``What does it really matter?"

"Your life."

"You don't have to worry about me or Lil BD," Boss told her.

"I'm sorry it has to be like this but I brought you in this world and I have to take your life just like I did Luc's," she said.

"No loyalty."

"Nope, but I want to introduce you to someone before I kill you." Janella pulled out a cell phone and called someone, telling them to come to the guest house.

"All this for what, Mom? You already had it all," Boss said.

"You never have enough power."

"So you used me, Lil BD, your dad, and your brothers to get to the top?"

"You'll understand one day," Janella said, as a White girl with red hair walked in and shared a deep passionate kiss with her. Boss never knew his mom was gay, and the red hair chick looked familiar. Then it came to him.

"Kylie!" Boss shouted, shocked to see Malik's ex-girlfriend there.

"Present!" 'Kylie raised her hand smiling.

"Kylie and I have been connected since the day I laid eyes on her. I'm the one who sent her to work for you at that car dealership you had in Chicago. I've always been bi-sexual. I like what I like, but Kylie just robbed all your drug spots in Chicago. I'ma let her take over Chicago," Janella said, slapping Kylie on her ass that had gotten extra phat.

"When Malik got killed by Lexus, my outlook on you changed, Boss. Bro's before hoes ... whatever happened to that? And he really loved you," Kylie said.

"Bitch, don't ever say his name," Boss told her.

"You about to die anyway so I'll let that slide, but you had a good run. Your mom planned all this out years ago. At first I said no it won't work, because I really thought you out of all people would catch on, but I guess she was right," Kylie looked at Janella's evil blush.

"I respect the thought put into it but at least I'll die with honor," Boss stated.

"Yes, you will, Son. I love you," Janella said.

Bloc! Bloc! Bloc! Bloc!

Janella shot Boss in the head four times as his body collapsed onto the glass table in slow motion,

"Let's fly out to Vegas," she told Kylie, grabbing the ass she'd got done four months ago.

When the door closed, Boss eyes opened up slowly and he felt glass stuck in his skin. He got up. He knew where Janella hid all of her weapons so he'd replaced all the real bullets with rubber bullets, just in case she'd tried to kill him.

He couldn't believe his mother was so ruthless and cold-hearted. He called Luc on the phone only to get his voicemail. Boss knew he had to leave before she got back. There was no turning back now, and Janella had just signed her own death warrant ...

To Be Continued...
Chi-Raq Gangstas 5
Coming Soon

Lock Down Publications and Ca$h Presents assisted publishing packages.

BASIC PACKAGE $499
Editing
Cover Design
Formatting

UPGRADED PACKAGE $800
Typing
Editing
Cover Design
Formatting

ADVANCE PACKAGE $1,200
Typing
Editing
Cover Design
Formatting
Copyright registration
Proofreading
Upload book to Amazon

LDP SUPREME PACKAGE $1,500
Typing
Editing
Cover Design
Formatting
Copyright registration
Proofreading
Set up Amazon account
Upload book to Amazon
Advertise on LDP Amazon and Facebook page

***Other services available upon request. Additional charges
may apply
Lock Down Publications
P.O. Box 944
Stockbridge, GA 30281-9998
Phone # 470 303-9761

Submission Guideline

Submit the first three chapters of your completed manuscript to ldpsubmissions@gmail.com, subject line: Your book's title. The manuscript must be in a .doc file and sent as an attachment. Document should be in Times New Roman, double spaced and in size 12 font. Also, provide your synopsis and full contact information. If sending multiple submissions, they must each be in a separate email.

Have a story but no way to send it electronically? You can still submit to LDP/Ca$h Presents. Send in the first three chapters, written or typed, of your completed manuscript to:

LDP: Submissions Dept
Po Box 944
Stockbridge, Ga 30281

DO NOT send original manuscript. Must be a duplicate.

Provide your synopsis and a cover letter containing your full contact information.

Thanks for considering LDP and Ca$h Presents.

NEW RELEASES

KING OF THE TRENCHES 3 by GHOST & TRANAY ADAMS

JACK BOYS VS DOPE BOYS 3 by ROMELL TUKES

LIFE OF A SAVAGE 4 by ROMELL TUKES

CHI'RAQ GANGSTAS 4 by ROMELL TUKES

Chi'Raq Gangstas 4

STRAIGHT BEAST MODE III

De'Kari

KINGPIN KILLAZ IV

STREET KINGS III

PAID IN BLOOD III

CARTEL KILLAZ IV

DOPE GODS III

Hood Rich

SINS OF A HUSTLA II

ASAD

RICH $AVAGE III

By Martell Troublesome Bolden

YAYO V

Bred In The Game 2

S. Allen

THE STREETS WILL TALK II

By Yolanda Moore

SON OF A DOPE FIEND III

HEAVEN GOT A GHETTO II

SKI MASK MONEY II

By Renta

LOYALTY AIN'T PROMISED III

By Keith Williams

I'M NOTHING WITHOUT HIS LOVE II

SINS OF A THUG II

TO THE THUG I LOVED BEFORE II

IN A HUSTLER I TRUST II

By Monet Dragun

QUIET MONEY IV

EXTENDED CLIP III

THUG LIFE IV
By **Trai'Quan**
THE STREETS MADE ME IV
By **Larry D. Wright**
IF YOU CROSS ME ONCE II
ANGEL IV
By **Anthony Fields**
THE STREETS WILL NEVER CLOSE IV
By K'ajji
HARD AND RUTHLESS III
KILLA KOUNTY III
By Khufu
MONEY GAME III
By Smoove Dolla
JACK BOYS VS DOPE BOYS IV
A GANGSTA'S QUR'AN V
COKE GIRLZ II
COKE BOYS II
LIFE OF A SAVAGE V
CHI'RAQ GANGSTAS V
By Romell Tukes
MURDA WAS THE CASE III
Elijah R. Freeman
THE STREETS NEVER LET GO III
By Robert Baptiste
AN UNFORESEEN LOVE IV
By **Meesha**

MONEY MAFIA II
By **Jibril Williams**

Chi'Raq Gangstas 4

QUEEN OF THE ZOO III

By Black Migo

VICIOUS LOYALTY III

By Kingpen

A GANGSTA'S PAIN III

By J-Blunt

CONFESSIONS OF A JACKBOY III

By Nicholas Lock

GRIMEY WAYS III

By Ray Vinci

KING KILLA II

By Vincent "Vitto" Holloway

BETRAYAL OF A THUG II

By Fre$h

THE MURDER QUEENS III

By Michael Gallon

THE BIRTH OF A GANGSTER III

By Delmont Player

TREAL LOVE II

By Le'Monica Jackson

FOR THE LOVE OF BLOOD II

By Jamel Mitchell

RAN OFF ON DA PLUG II

By Paper Boi Rari

HOOD CONSIGLIERE II

By Keese

PRETTY GIRLS DO NASTY THINGS II

By Nicole Goosby

PROTÉGÉ OF A LEGEND II

By Corey Robinson

Romell Tukes

IT'S JUST ME AND YOU II
By Ah'Million
BORN IN THE GRAVE II
By Self Made Tay
FOREVER GANGSTA III
By Adrian Dulan
GORILLAZ IN THE TRENCHES II
By SayNoMore

Available Now

RESTRAINING ORDER **I & II**
By **CA$H & Coffee**
LOVE KNOWS NO BOUNDARIES **I II & III**
By **Coffee**
RAISED AS A GOON I, II, III & IV
BRED BY THE SLUMS I, II, III
BLAST FOR ME I & II
ROTTEN TO THE CORE I II III
A BRONX TALE I, II, III
DUFFLE BAG CARTEL I II III IV V VI
HEARTLESS GOON I II III IV V
A SAVAGE DOPEBOY I II
DRUG LORDS I II III

214

Chi'Raq Gangstas 4

CUTTHROAT MAFIA I II
KING OF THE TRENCHES
By **Ghost**
LAY IT DOWN **I & II**
LAST OF A DYING BREED I II
BLOOD STAINS OF A SHOTTA I & II III
By **Jamaica**
LOYAL TO THE GAME I II III
LIFE OF SIN I, II III
By **TJ & Jelissa**
BLOODY COMMAS I & II
SKI MASK CARTEL I II & III
KING OF NEW YORK I II,III IV V
RISE TO POWER I II III
COKE KINGS I II III IV V
BORN HEARTLESS I II III IV
KING OF THE TRAP I II
By **T.J. Edwards**
IF LOVING HIM IS WRONG...I & II
LOVE ME EVEN WHEN IT HURTS I II III
By **Jelissa**
WHEN THE STREETS CLAP BACK I & II III
THE HEART OF A SAVAGE I II III IV
MONEY MAFIA
LOYAL TO THE SOIL I II III
By **Jibril Williams**
A DISTINGUISHED THUG STOLE MY HEART I II & III
LOVE SHOULDN'T HURT I II III IV
RENEGADE BOYS I II III IV
PAID IN KARMA I II III

Romell Tukes

SAVAGE STORMS I II III

AN UNFORESEEN LOVE I II III

By **Meesha**

A GANGSTER'S CODE I &, II III

A GANGSTER'S SYN I II III

THE SAVAGE LIFE I II III

CHAINED TO THE STREETS I II III

BLOOD ON THE MONEY I II III

A GANGSTA'S PAIN I II

By J-Blunt

PUSH IT TO THE LIMIT

By **Bre' Hayes**

BLOOD OF A BOSS **I, II, III, IV, V**

SHADOWS OF THE GAME

TRAP BASTARD

By **Askari**

THE STREETS BLEED MURDER **I, II & III**

THE HEART OF A GANGSTA I II& III

By **Jerry Jackson**

CUM FOR ME I II III IV V VI VII VIII

An **LDP Erotica Collaboration**

BRIDE OF A HUSTLA **I II & II**

THE FETTI GIRLS **I, II& III**

CORRUPTED BY A GANGSTA I, II III, IV

BLINDED BY HIS LOVE

THE PRICE YOU PAY FOR LOVE I, II ,III

DOPE GIRL MAGIC I II III

By **Destiny Skai**

WHEN A GOOD GIRL GOES BAD

By **Adrienne**

THE COST OF LOYALTY I II III

By Kweli

A GANGSTER'S REVENGE **I II III & IV**

THE BOSS MAN'S DAUGHTERS I II III IV V

A SAVAGE LOVE **I & II**

BAE BELONGS TO ME I II

A HUSTLER'S DECEIT I, II, III

WHAT BAD BITCHES DO I, II, III

SOUL OF A MONSTER I II III

KILL ZONE

A DOPE BOY'S QUEEN I II III

TIL DEATH

By **Aryanna**

A KINGPIN'S AMBITON

A KINGPIN'S AMBITION **II**

I MURDER FOR THE DOUGH

By **Ambitious**

TRUE SAVAGE I II III IV V VI VII

DOPE BOY MAGIC I, II, III

MIDNIGHT CARTEL I II III

CITY OF KINGZ I II

NIGHTMARE ON SILENT AVE

THE PLUG OF LIL MEXICO II

CLASSIC CITY

By **Chris Green**

A DOPEBOY'S PRAYER

By **Eddie "Wolf" Lee**

THE KING CARTEL **I, II & III**

By **Frank Gresham**

THESE NIGGAS AIN'T LOYAL **I, II & III**

Romell Tukes

By **Nikki Tee**
GANGSTA SHYT **I II &III**
By **CATO**
THE ULTIMATE BETRAYAL
By **Phoenix**
BOSS'N UP **I , II & III**
By **Royal Nicole**
I LOVE YOU TO DEATH
By **Destiny J**
I RIDE FOR MY HITTA
I STILL RIDE FOR MY HITTA
By **Misty Holt**
LOVE & CHASIN' PAPER
By **Qay Crockett**
TO DIE IN VAIN
SINS OF A HUSTLA
By **ASAD**
BROOKLYN HUSTLAZ
By **Boogsy Morina**
BROOKLYN ON LOCK I & II
By **Sonovia**
GANGSTA CITY
By **Teddy Duke**
A DRUG KING AND HIS DIAMOND I & II III
A DOPEMAN'S RICHES
HER MAN, MINE'S TOO I, II
CASH MONEY HO'S
THE WIFEY I USED TO BE I II
PRETTY GIRLS DO NASTY THINGS
By Nicole Goosby

218

Chi'Raq Gangstas 4

TRAPHOUSE KING **I II & III**

KINGPIN KILLAZ I II III

STREET KINGS I II

PAID IN BLOOD **I II**

CARTEL KILLAZ I II III

DOPE GODS I II

By **Hood Rich**

LIPSTICK KILLAH **I, II, III**

CRIME OF PASSION I II & III

FRIEND OR FOE I II III

By **Mimi**

STEADY MOBBN' **I, II, III**

THE STREETS STAINED MY SOUL I II III

By **Marcellus Allen**

WHO SHOT YA **I, II, III**

SON OF A DOPE FIEND I II

HEAVEN GOT A GHETTO

SKI MASK MONEY

Renta

GORILLAZ IN THE BAY **I II III IV**

TEARS OF A GANGSTA I II

3X KRAZY I II

STRAIGHT BEAST MODE I II

DE'KARI

TRIGGADALE I II III

MURDAROBER WAS THE CASE I II

Elijah R. Freeman

GOD BLESS THE TRAPPERS I, II, III

THESE SCANDALOUS STREETS I, II, III

FEAR MY GANGSTA I, II, III IV, V

Romell Tukes

THESE STREETS DON'T LOVE NOBODY I, II

BURY ME A G I, II, III, IV, V

A GANGSTA'S EMPIRE I, II, III, IV

THE DOPEMAN'S BODYGAURD I II

THE REALEST KILLAZ I II III

THE LAST OF THE OGS I II III

Tranay Adams

THE STREETS ARE CALLING

Duquie Wilson

MARRIED TO A BOSS I II III

By Destiny Skai & Chris Green

KINGZ OF THE GAME I II III IV V VI

Playa Ray

SLAUGHTER GANG I II III

RUTHLESS HEART I II III

By Willie Slaughter

FUK SHYT

By Blakk Diamond

DON'T F#CK WITH MY HEART I II

By Linnea

ADDICTED TO THE DRAMA I II III

IN THE ARM OF HIS BOSS II

By Jamila

YAYO I II III IV

A SHOOTER'S AMBITION I II

BRED IN THE GAME

By S. Allen

TRAP GOD I II III

RICH $AVAGE I II

MONEY IN THE GRAVE I II III

220

Chi'Raq Gangstas 4

By Martell Troublesome Bolden
FOREVER GANGSTA I II
GLOCKS ON SATIN SHEETS I II
By Adrian Dulan
TOE TAGZ I II III IV
LEVELS TO THIS SHYT I II
IT'S JUST ME AND YOU
By Ah'Million
KINGPIN DREAMS I II III
RAN OFF ON DA PLUG
By Paper Boi Rari
CONFESSIONS OF A GANGSTA I II III IV
CONFESSIONS OF A JACKBOY I II
By Nicholas Lock
I'M NOTHING WITHOUT HIS LOVE
SINS OF A THUG
TO THE THUG I LOVED BEFORE
A GANGSTA SAVED XMAS
IN A HUSTLER I TRUST
By Monet Dragun
CAUGHT UP IN THE LIFE I II III
THE STREETS NEVER LET GO I II
By Robert Baptiste
NEW TO THE GAME I II III
MONEY, MURDER & MEMORIES I II III
By **Malik D. Rice**
LIFE OF A SAVAGE I II III IV
A GANGSTA'S QUR'AN I II III IV
MURDA SEASON I II III
GANGLAND CARTEL I II III

Romell Tukes

CHI'RAQ GANGSTAS I II III IV

KILLERS ON ELM STREET I II III

JACK BOYZ N DA BRONX I II III

A DOPEBOY'S DREAM I II III

JACK BOYS VS DOPE BOYS I II III

COKE GIRLZ

COKE BOYS

By Romell Tukes

LOYALTY AIN'T PROMISED I II

By Keith Williams

QUIET MONEY I II III

THUG LIFE I II III

EXTENDED CLIP I II

A GANGSTA'S PARADISE

By **Trai'Quan**

THE STREETS MADE ME I II III

By **Larry D. Wright**

THE ULTIMATE SACRIFICE I, II, III, IV, V, VI

KHADIFI

IF YOU CROSS ME ONCE

ANGEL I II III

IN THE BLINK OF AN EYE

By **Anthony Fields**

THE LIFE OF A HOOD STAR

By Ca$h & Rashia Wilson

THE STREETS WILL NEVER CLOSE I II III

By K'ajji

CREAM I II III

THE STREETS WILL TALK

By Yolanda Moore

222

NIGHTMARES OF A HUSTLA I II III

By King Dream

CONCRETE KILLA I II III

VICIOUS LOYALTY I II

By Kingpen

HARD AND RUTHLESS I II

MOB TOWN 251

THE BILLIONAIRE BENTLEYS I II III

By Von Diesel

GHOST MOB

Stilloan Robinson

MOB TIES I II III IV V VI

SOUL OF A HUSTLER, HEART OF A KILLER

GORILLAZ IN THE TRENCHES

By SayNoMore

BODYMORE MURDERLAND I II III

THE BIRTH OF A GANGSTER I II

By Delmont Player

FOR THE LOVE OF A BOSS

By C. D. Blue

MOBBED UP I II III IV

THE BRICK MAN I II III IV

THE COCAINE PRINCESS I II III IV V

By King Rio

KILLA KOUNTY I II III

By Khufu

MONEY GAME I II

By Smoove Dolla

A GANGSTA'S KARMA I II

By FLAME

Romell Tukes

KING OF THE TRENCHES I II III
by **GHOST & TRANAY ADAMS**
QUEEN OF THE ZOO I II
By **Black Migo**
GRIMEY WAYS I II
By Ray Vinci
XMAS WITH AN ATL SHOOTER
By Ca$h & Destiny Skai
KING KILLA
By Vincent "Vitto" Holloway
BETRAYAL OF A THUG
By Fre$h
THE MURDER QUEENS I II
By Michael Gallon
TREAL LOVE
By Le'Monica Jackson
FOR THE LOVE OF BLOOD
By Jamel Mitchell
HOOD CONSIGLIERE
By Keese
PROTÉGÉ OF A LEGEND
By Corey Robinson
BORN IN THE GRAVE
By Self Made Tay
MOAN IN MY MOUTH
By XTASY

<u>BOOKS BY LDP'S CEO, CA$H</u>

TRUST IN NO MAN
TRUST IN NO MAN 2
TRUST IN NO MAN 3
BONDED BY BLOOD
SHORTY GOT A THUG
THUGS CRY
THUGS CRY 2
THUGS CRY 3
TRUST NO BITCH
TRUST NO BITCH 2
TRUST NO BITCH 3
TIL MY CASKET DROPS
RESTRAINING ORDER
RESTRAINING ORDER 2
IN LOVE WITH A CONVICT
LIFE OF A HOOD STAR
XMAS WITH AN ATL SHOOTER

Romell Tukes